PSI HIGH AND OTHERS

Psi High

AND OTHERS

---

by ALAN E. NOURSE

FABER AND FABER
24 Russell Square
London

First published in Great Britain in mcmlxviii
by Faber and Faber Limited
24 Russell Square London WC1
Printed in Great Britain by
Latimer Trend & Co Ltd Whitstable
All rights reserved

For Jim, Doreen
and Cynthia

Contents

PSI HIGH AND OTHERS

Prologue

For FOURTEEN DAYS, by Earth reckoning, the outpost ship of the Watchers patiently continued in its orbit, circling the great planet called Jupiter like a silent shadow, waiting for some sign of Kadar's return.

The ship had come silently from halfway across the Galaxy, responding to a prearranged call signal. Now it was here, an undetected visitor to this remote solar province with its dwarf yellow star and its ten obscure planets. It was not the first time an outpost ship had come here, although visits had been relatively infrequent in the time since life had first appeared on the third planet of this star. Many in the Confederation—especially those with short memories—had opposed surveillance of such a backwater region at all, but the Watchers as usual had prevailed. They knew from long experience that it was not the remoteness of a new-appearing race that mattered, but its intelligence and its potential to build—or to destroy—the Confederation in the future. Once a people had broken free from the star that spawned them, remoteness was no longer a consideration. But the nature of the people was something else.

Now, as the outpost ship swung in its orbit, no ray of sunlight reflected from its surface. No radar signal bounced back to reveal even a shadow. The physical substance of the ship and the two Watchers aboard it were such that no radiant energy could be reflected; indeed, if an Earth ship were to come into collision course with the Watchers it would pass right through and beyond them without so much as a hint that a "collision" had occurred. It was necessary, under the Covenant, that the Watchers remain undetected, and the Covenant had not been violated in all the tens of thousands of years that these ships had been regular visitors to this solar system. When contact *had* been made with these developing Earthmen, its true nature had always been concealed, just as the Covenant demanded.

And now the Watchers were waiting for the end of one such contact.

Of the two aboard the craft, only the younger was impatient. "Why so long?" he asked with increasing urgency. "He called for the rendezvous himself. Why does he keep us waiting? What could have gone wrong?"

The Old One sighed. Service with a Young One fresh from the academy was always more trial than joy. The eager textbook knowledge of the Covenant and its surveillance procedures were fine, but there was no experience to modulate all this frantic energy, and above all, no patience. "Nothing has gone wrong," the Old One said. "Kadar will come, but he dare not just disappear from their midst for no reason. It must be done in the proper way, and that takes time."

"But so *much* time!" the Young One said. "Fourteen of their days, and no end in sight."

"And this is so much time? After watching these stubborn people for millennia?" The Old One smiled. "Of course you're eager to be gone; so am I. But consider Kadar's problem scientifically."

The Young One caught the gentle note of reproach. "Very well, sir. If you will instruct me."

"Just consider: his departure would have to appear consistent with the way Earth people take leave of things—a 'death,' so to speak—but it must also appear quite unremarkable. Not too dramatic a demise, nothing too abrupt or too tragic. And in particular, nothing even to hint of foul play. Their people at the Hoffman Medical Center are not fools. And then, with his 'death' accomplished, there would be still further delay. For all their advancement, Earth people still cling to certain long-revered rituals. Funerals, for instance."

The Old One turned back to the space scanner as his young apprentice thought about this. Finally the Young One said, "Of course, I know they have come a long way, these Earthmen, but there are still many things I do not see. Why now, after all this time, are we ending our surveillance?"

"Because the time has come to withdraw," the Old One said.

"How do we know? Has the Confederation already reached a decision?"

"Not yet. But it will, as soon as we return."

"How *can* they, when we know so little about these creatures?"

"We know more about them than you think," the Old One said. "It isn't the quantity of data that makes the difference, it's the *quality*. And basically, a decision for or against quarantine and possible imprisonment hangs upon one question: will these people one day become peaceful and productive partners in the Galactic Confederation, or will they become a malignancy in our midst that must then, too late, be confronted and expunged? There was one such malignant race, if you recall your history. They had many qualities in common with these

Earthmen in their early days, and it took a million years of warfare to stop them. The Confederation cannot allow another such race the freedom to expand."

"And you think a decision can be reached so soon?" the Young One asked. "Oh, I know that all the known intelligent races have followed certain patterns. Always they have been aggressive. Always they have been curious. Always they have fought their own wars, and always they have learned to control mass-energy conversion. But how can the future be predicted from these things early enough to do any good?"

"It can't," the Old One replied. "But those parts of the pattern don't matter in the long run. You've ignored the three factors that *do* matter, the three things we *had to know* about these Earthmen before a decision could even be possible. How they deal with nuclear energy is none of our concern. How they—or any race—deal with three other key universal problems is very much our concern, and a valid basis for predicting what the future holds."

"And those three problems?"

"The obvious ones. How they use their growing knowledge of their own physiology and biochemistry, for healthy growth or for destruction. How they deal with their own evolutionary development, especially when the higher extrasensory powers begin to appear, as they always do. How they handle their first encounters with other intelligent creatures. Simple enough things, yet utterly crucial, because *the solutions they find mold the pattern of their future.*"

The Old One turned once again to scan the void of space around them. "That is why we came to this remote region in the first place: because intelligent life had appeared here and we had to know what solutions they found. With these people it has been easy. They've developed so very fast, for one thing; no other race in history has ever scrambled up as urgently as these people have. Which could make them all the more dangerous, of course, if they found the wrong solutions. In addition, they have always had a burgeoning curiosity about their own minds and bodies; and recently a single research organization, their so-called Hoffman Center, has been deeply involved in all three of the areas we have been watching. Useful, for us. A single observation post from which we could follow all three lines of development."

The Old One leaned back, smiling at his young companion. "So now the data is collected. Kadar will bring nothing new with him when he comes. Our tapes and records here already tell the whole story; perhaps you should review them again, while we wait. You might see then why our surveillance is over. And perhaps—" he paused, thinking once again of the three particular crises that he himself had witnessed among these Earthmen during his long centuries as Watcher here—"perhaps you will even see what the decision must ultimately be."

PART ONE

The Martyr

1

F OUR AND one-half hours after Martian
sunset, the last light in the Headquarters Building finally
flicked out.

Carl Golden stamped his feet against the cold, blowing into
his cupped hands to warm them as he pressed back into the
shadow of the doorway across from Headquarters. The night
air bit his nostrils and turned his breath into clouds of grey
vapor in the semidarkness. The atmosphere screens surrounding the Ironstone Colony on Mars kept the oxygen in, all right,
but they could never keep the biting cold out. After this long
vigil he was chilled to the bone and bored to the point of
screaming, but when the light at last went out across the way,
boredom vanished and warm blood prickled through his shiv-
ering legs.

He slid back tight against the coarse black stone of the doorway, peering intently across the road into the gloom. Who had
been staying so late? The girl, of course. He'd thought so,

but wasn't sure until he saw her coming out, heard the faint chink of keys as she pulled the heavy door down on its counter-weights behind her and locked it. A quick glance left and right, and she started down the frosty road toward the lights of the colony.

Carl Golden waited until she was out of sight. No briefcase; good, good. That was one loophole he had thought of while he stood there freezing. Not that *anybody* took any work home around here, but there was always a chance. His heart pounded as he forced himself to wait ten minutes more; then, teeth chattering in the cold, he ducked swiftly across the dark road to the low, one-story building.

Through the window he could see the lobby call-board. All the lights were dark. Good, again—no one remained in the lower levels. Headquarters ran by routine, just like everything else in this god-forsaken hole. Utter, abysmal, trancelike routine. The girl had been a little later than usual, but that was because of the supply ship coming in tomorrow, no doubt. Reports to get ready, supply requisitions to fill out, personnel recommendations to complete—

—*and the final reports on Armstrong's death. Mustn't forget that, Carl. The real story, the absolute, factual truth, without any nonsense. The reports that would go, ultimately, to Walter Rinehart and to no one else, just as all the other important reports from the Ironstone Colony had been going for so many years. Only this time Walter Rinehart was in for a surprise.*

Carl skirted the long, low building, clinging to the black shadows of the side wall. Halfway around he came to the supply chute, covered with a heavy moulded-stone cover.

Now?

It had to be now, and this was the only way; it had taken four endless months here for him to discover that. Four months of this ridiculous masquerade, made all the more idiotic by the fact that every soul in the colony had accepted him for exactly what he pretended to be, and never once challenged him; not even Terry Fisher, who habitually challenged everything and everybody, even when he was sober! But the four months of play-acting had told on Carl's nerves; they showed in his reactions, in the hollows under his sharp brown eyes. The specter of a slip-up, an aroused suspicion, was always in his mind, and he knew that until he had the reports before his eyes, there was nothing Dan Fowler could do to save him if he betrayed himself. The night he'd left Earth, Dan had shaken his hand and said, "Remember, lad, I don't know you. Sorry it's got to be that way, but we can't risk it now." And they couldn't, of course. Not until they knew, for certain, who had murdered Kenneth Armstrong.

They already knew why.

The utter stillness of the place reassured him; he hoisted up the chute cover, threw it high, and worked his long legs and body into the chute. It was a steep slide downwards; he held his breath for an instant, listening, then let go. Blackness engulfed him as the cover snapped closed behind him. He went down fast, struck hard and rolled. The chute opened into the commissary in the third deep-level of the building; the place was as black as the inside of a pocket. He tested unbroken legs with a sigh of relief, then limped around crates and boxes in the darkness to the place where the door ought to be.

In the corridor beyond there was some light—dim phosphorescence from the Martian night-rock lining the walls and tiling the floor. Carl walked swiftly, aware of the deafening clack-clack of his heels on the ringing stone. At the end of the corridor he tried the heavy door.

It complained, but it gave. Carl sighed his relief. It had been a quick, imperfect job of jimmying the lock; he had left it looking so obviously tampered with that he'd worried about it all day. But then, why would anyone test it? Unless they suspected a snake in their midst—

Through the door he stepped into a black room again, started forward as the door swung shut behind him. Then somewhere a shoe scraped, the faintest rustle of sound. Carl froze. His own trouser leg? A trick of acoustics? He didn't move a muscle.

Silence. Then: "Carl?"

His pocket light flickered around the room, revealing a secretary's cubbyhole, a typewriter. It stopped on a pair of trouser legs, a body, slouched down in the soft plastifoam chair, a sleepy face, ruddy and bland, with a shock of sandy hair and quizzical eyebrows.

"*Terry!* What are you doing here in the dark?"

"Waiting for you, old boy." The man leaned forward, grinning up at him. "You're late, Carl. Should have made it sooner than this, sheems—seems to me."

Carl's light moved past the man in the chair to the floor. The bottle was standing there, barely half full. "You're drunk," he said.

"Course I'm drunk," Terry Fisher laughed. "You think I was going to sober up after you left me at that bar tonight? No thanks, I'd rather be drunk, any day of the week, around this dump."

"Well, you've got to get out of here, go get drunk somewhere else." Carl's voice rose in bitter anger. Of all times, of *all* times—"Terry, how did you get in here? You've *got* to get out."

The man looked up, no longer laughing. "So do you. They're on to you, Carl. I don't think you know that, but they are." He leaned forward precariously. "I had a talk with Barness this morning, one of his nice 'spontaneous' chats, and he pumped the hell out of me and thought I was too drunk to know what he was doing. They're expecting you to come here tonight—"

Carl tugged at the drunken man's arm in the darkness. "Get *out* of here, Terry, or so help me—"

Terry clutched at him. "Didn't you hear me? They *know* about you. They know you're no personnel supervisor. Barness thinks you're spying for the Asian Bloc. They're starting a Mars colony too, you know. Barness is sure you're selling them information."

"Barness is an ass," Carl said.

"Of course, just like all the other Retreads they have running this place," Terry said, "but *I'm* not an ass, and you didn't fool me for two days."

Carl gritted his teeth. How could Terry Fisher know? "For the last time—"

Fisher lurched to his feet. "Look, friend, they'll *get* you if you don't go. They can try you and shoot you right on the spot, and Barness will do it, too. I had to warn you that you've walked right into it, but you can still get away—"

It was hateful but there was no other way. The drunken man's head jerked up at the blow, and he gave a little grunt, then slid back down on the chair. Carl checked his pulse, then scrambled over his legs and headed for the vault door beyond. If they caught him *now*, Terry Fisher was right, they could shoot him on the spot. But give him five more minutes—

The lock squeaked, and the vault door fell open. Inside he tore through the file cases, wrenched at the locker drawers in frantic haste, ripping the weak aluminum sheeting like thick tinfoil. Then he found the folder with KENNETH ARM-STRONG marked on the tab.

Somewhere above him an alarm went off, screaming a mournful note through the building. He threw on the light switch, flooding the room with whiteness, and started through the papers in the folder one by one. No time to read what the papers said, a one-second look at each sheet was enough. Retinal photos were hard to superimpose swiftly and keep straight, but that was one reason why Carl Golden was on Mars right now instead of sitting in some office back on Earth.

He scanned the last page, and threw the folder onto the floor. As he went through the door, he flipped out the light, raced with clattering footsteps down the corridor.

Lights caught him from both sides, slicing the blackness like hot knives. *"All right, Golden. Stop right there."*

Dark figures came out of the lights, ripped his clothing off without a word. Somebody wrenched open his mouth, shined a light in, rammed coarse cold fingers into his throat. There was a smell of sweat, and harsh, angry whispers. Then: "All right, you snake, upstairs. Barness wants to see you."

They packed him naked into the street, hurried him into a three-wheeled ground car. Five minutes later he was herded out of the car into another building, and Barness, the Ironstone administrator, was glaring at him across the room.

Odd things flashed through Carl's mind. You seldom saw a Retread really get angry, but Barness was angry. The man's young-old face (the strange, utterly ageless amalgamation of sixty years of wisdom, superimposed by the youth of a twenty-year-old) had unaccustomed lines of wrath about the eyes and mouth. Barness didn't waste words. "What were you after down there?"

"Armstrong." Carl cut the word out almost gleefully. "And I got what I wanted, and there's nothing you or Walter Rinehart or anybody else can do about it now. I don't know *what* I saw in that report, but I've got it recorded in my eyes and in my brain now and you can't touch it."

"You stupid fool, we can *peel* your brain," Barness snarled.

"Well, you won't. You won't dare."

Barness glanced at the officer who had brought him in. "Jack—"

"Senator Dan Fowler won't like it," said Carl.

The administrator stopped short, blinking at him. He took a slow breath. Then he sank down into his chair. "Fowler," he said, as though dawn was just breaking.

"That's right. Dan Fowler sent me up here. I've found what he wants. You shoot me now, and when they probe you, Dan will know that I found it, and you won't be around for another rejuvenation."

Barness looked suddenly old, and puzzled. "But what did he *want?*"

"The truth about Kenneth Armstrong's death. Not the 'accident' story you fed to the TVs—Tragic End for World Hero, Died with His Boots On, and all that twaddle. Dan wanted the truth. Who killed him. Why this colony is grinding down from compound low to stop, and turning men like Terry Fisher into alcoholic bums. Why Ironstone is turning into a superrefined Birdie's Rest for old men. But mostly who killed Armstrong, how he was murdered, who gave the orders. And if you don't mind, I'd like my clothes back, I'm getting cold."

"And you got all that," said Barness, wonderingly.

"That's right."

"But you haven't *read* what you got, have you?"

"Not yet. Plenty of time for that on the way back."

Barness nodded wearily, and tossed Carl his clothes. "Maybe you ought to read it tonight. It might just surprise you."

Golden's eyes widened. Something in the man's voice, some curious note of defeat and hopelessness, told him that Barness was not lying. "Really? In what way?"

"Armstrong's death wasn't accidental, you're right there. We lied to the press about that. But nobody murdered him, either. Nobody gave any orders, to anybody. Nobody wanted him dead. The reason Armstrong died was because he shot himself—quite of his own volition."

2

"ALL RIGHT, Senator," the young red-headed doctor said. "You told me you wanted it straight. That's how you're going to get it." Moments before, Dr. Moss had been laughing and joking in pleasant banter. He wasn't laughing now. "You've got six months, at the outside. Nine, if you went to bed tomorrow, retired from the Senate, and lived on tea and crackers. But from where I'm sitting I wouldn't bet a plugged nickel that you'll be alive a month from now. If you think I'm joking, you just try to squeeze a bet out of me."

Senator Dan Fowler took the black cigar from his mouth, stared at the chewed-up end for a moment, and put it back in his mouth. There was something exceedingly witty that he'd planned to say at this point in the examination, but now it didn't seem too funny. If Dr. Moss had been some mealy-mouthed quack like some of the doctors Dan had seen, it would be easy. But Dr. Moss wasn't. He was one of the very sharp, very competent, very human doctors the Hoffman Medical Center had been training in these past few decades, among the best doctors you could find in the world. Furthermore, Dr. Moss did not seem overwhelmingly impressed by the man sitting across the desk from him, senator or no senator, a fact which made Dan Fowler just a trifle uneasy. He looked at the doctor and scowled. "Garbage," he said.

The red-headed doctor shrugged. "Look, Senator, sometimes a banana is a banana. I know heart disease, and I know how it acts. I also know it kills people if they wait too long. And once you're dead, no rejuvenation lab is going to bring you back to life."

"Oh, hell! Who's dying?" Fowler's grey eyebrows knit in

the old familiar scowl, and he bit down hard on the cigar. "Heart disease! So I get a little pain now and then—it never lasts long, and when it starts getting bad I'll come in and take the full treatment. But I can't do it now!" He spread his hands in a violent gesture. "I only came in here because my daughter dragged me. My heart's doing fine. I've been working an eighteen-hour day for forty years now, and I can do it for another year or two."

"But you do have pain," Dr. Moss said gently.

"So? A little twinge, now and then."

"Like whenever you lose your temper. Whenever you run for a plane. Whenever anything upsets you."

"All right—a twinge."

"Which makes you sit down for ten or fifteen minutes when it comes on, and doesn't go away any more with just one nitro tablet, you have to take two, and sometimes three—right?"

Dan Fowler blinked. "All right, sometimes it gets a little bad—"

"And it used to be only once or twice a month, but now it's almost every day. And once or twice you've just blacked out for a while, and made your staff work like demons to cover for you and keep it off the TV, right?"

"Say, who's been talking to you?"

"Really, Senator!"

"Can't even trust your own blood daughter to keep her trap shut." Fowler tossed his cigar butt down in disgust. "It happened once, yes. That confounded Rinehart is enough to make *anybody* black out." He thrust out his jaw and glowered at Dr. Moss as though it were all *his* fault. Then he grinned. "Oh, I know you're right, Doc, it's just that this is the wrong *time*. I can't take two months out now. There's too much to be done between now and the middle of next month."

"Oh, yes. The Hearings. Why not turn them over to your staff? They know what's going on."

"Nonsense. They know, but not like I know. After the Hearings, fine. I'll come along like a lamb. But right now—"

Dr. Moss reddened, slammed his fist down on the desk. "Senator, are you both blind and deaf? Or just plain stupid? Didn't you hear me a moment ago? *You may not live through the Hearings.* You could go out, just like that, any minute. But this is 2134 A.D., not the Middle Ages. It would be so utterly, hopelessly pointless to let that happen."

Fowler champed his cigar and scowled. "After the Retread was done I'd have to free-agent for a year, wouldn't I?" It was an accusation.

"You *should*. But that's really only a formality. If you want to go right back to the same thing you were doing before you came to the center, that's purely your option."

"Yes, *if!* But supposing I didn't? Supposing I was all changed."

The young doctor looked at the man shrewdly. Dan Fowler was fifty-six years old and he looked forty. It seemed incredible even to Dr. Moss that this man could have done what he had done, and still look almost as young and fighting-mad now as he had when he started. Clever old goat, too, but Dan Fowler's last remarks had lifted a veil. Moss smiled to himself. "You're afraid of it, aren't you, Senator?"

"Of rejuvenation? Nonsense."

"But you are. You aren't the only one, it's a pretty frightening thing. Cash in the old model, take out a new one, just like a jet racer or a worn out talk-writer. Only it isn't machinery, it's your body, and your life." Dr. Moss spread his hands. "It scares a man. *Rejuvenation* isn't the right word, of course. Aside from the neurones, they take away every cell in your body, one way or another, and give you new ones. A hundred and fifty years ago Cancelmo and Klein did it on a dog, right in this building when the Hoffman Center was new. They called it *subtotal prosthesis*. A crude job—I've studied their papers and films. Vat-grown hearts and kidneys, revitalized vascular material, building up new organ systems like a patchwork quilt, coaxing new tissues to grow to replace old ones. But they got a living dog out of it, and that dog lived to the ripe old age of thirty-seven years."

Dr. Moss pushed back from his desk, watching Dan Fowler's face. "Then in 1992 Nimrock tried it on a Mercy Man here, and almost got himself convicted of murder because the man died. That was a hundred and forty-one years ago. While Nimrock's trial was still going on, his workers completed the second job, and the man *lived,* and oh, did that jury fall over itself to have Nimrock set free!"

As the doctor talked, Dan Fowler sat silent, chewing his cigar furiously. But listening—he was listening, all right. "Well, it was a crude process in those days," Dr. Moss said. "Hit or miss. But in those days the Hoffman Center was barely getting organized as a great medical research complex. They were still using Mercy Men—paid medical mercenaries—for their experiments, and public opinion was fighting them like mad. With rejuvenation a success, they brought in the best researchers and clinical physicians the world had to offer, threw everything they had into it, with more financial support than they knew what to do with, and today there is nothing crude or haphazard about subtotal prosthesis." He pointed to a bronze plaque hanging on the wall. "That's on the wall of every examining room here in the Hoffman Center. You've seen it before; read it."

Dan Fowler's eyes went up to the plaque. A list of names. At the top words said, *"These ten gave life to Mankind."*

Below it were the names:

Martin Aronson, Ph.D.	Education
Thomas Bevalaqua	Literature and Art
Chauncey Devlin	Music

Frederick A. Kehler, M.S.	Engineering
William B. Morse, L.L.D.	Law
Rev. John McFarlane	Philosophy and Theology
Jacob Prowsnitz, Ph.D.	History
John W. Shaw, M.D.	Medicine
Carlotta Sokol, Ph.D.	Sociopsychology
Harvey Tatum	Business

"I know," said Dan Fowler. "June 1, 2005. They were the first scientifically controlled volunteers."

"Ten out of several thousand volunteers," Moss amended. "Those ten were chosen by lot. Already people were dreaming about what subtotal prosthesis could do. Think of it, at a time when death by the age of eighty or ninety was still a virtual certainty, and very final too! To preserve the great minds, compound the accumulated wisdom of one lifetime with still another lifetime, and maybe another and another—the old Fountain of Youth dream, at last come true! So those ten people, representing ten great fields of study, volunteered to risk their lives. Not to live forever, just to see if rejuvenation really *could* preserve their minds in newly built bodies. All of them were old, older than you are, Senator. Some were sicker than you are, and believe me, every one of them was afraid. But seven of the ten are *still alive today*, a hundred and thirty years later. John Shaw died in a jet crash ten years after his first Retread. Tatum died of a neuro-toxic virus, because in those days we couldn't do anything to rebuild neurones and brain tissue. Bevalaqua took his own life, for reasons unknown. The rest are still alive, vigorously and productively alive, after two more rejuvenations."

"Fine," said Dan Fowler. "I still can't do it now."

"That was just ten people," Dr. Moss cut in. "It took five years to get ready for them, then. Today we can handle five *hundred* a year, but still only five hundred select individuals, to live on instead of dying. You have the incredible good fortune to be one of those chosen, and you've got the gall to sit there and tell me you don't have the time for it!"

The senator rose slowly, lighting another cigar. "Doctor, it could be five *thousand* a year instead of five hundred. That's why I don't have the time. It could be fifteen thousand, *fifty* thousand. It could be, but it's not. Senator Walter Rinehart has been rejuvenated twice already. He is one of the most corrupt politicians this nation has ever spawned, the chairman of the committee that makes the final, irrevocable selection of just exactly who the lucky ones will be each year. Rinehart's on the list, of course. *I'm* on the list because I've shouted so loudly and made such a stink for such a long time that the Criterion Committee didn't dare leave me off. But *you're* not on the list. Why not? You could be. Every productive individual in our society *could* be."

Dr. Moss spread his hands. "I'm not beefing. The Criterion Committee does the choosing."

"Rinehart's criteria!" Dan Fowler exploded.

"But Rinehart doesn't decide for himself. There are all sorts of wise men and women on that committee, people trained in every area of knowledge, working themselves sick to pick out the best choices each year."

Fowler looked at him. "Yes, working to pick out who shall live and who shall not live. Well, who is wise enough for *that* job? You don't know very much about people, Doctor. Nor about politics. Who do you think set the figure at five hundred a year? The Hoffman Center? The committee? No. Rinehart set the number. Who has consistently maneuvered to hold down appropriations so the center couldn't handle more than five hundred? Rinehart has, seven times, now. The committeemen are good people, but they want to live, too, and their chairman is a vulture. For decades he's used the Criterion Committee as his own personal weapon. Built power with it.

Got it in a strangle hold he never intends to let go." The senator leaned across the desk, his eyes bright with anger. "I haven't time to stop for a Retread now, because finally, at last, I *can* stop Walter Rinehart, if only I can live a few more weeks. I can break him, free the Criterion Committee from his control, or any one man's control, *now* while there's still a chance, and throw rejuvenation open to everybody instead of to five hundred chosen ones a year. I can stop Rinehart because I've dug at him and dug at him for twenty-nine years, and shouted and screamed and fought and made people listen, and now, finally, I have him boxed into a corner that he can't get out of. And if I fumble *now,* it'll all be down the drain, finished, washed up. And if that happens, *nobody* will ever be able to stop him."

There was silence in the little examining room. Then Dr. Moss spread his hands. "The Hearings are that critical, eh?"

"I'm afraid they are."

"But why does it have to be your personal fight? Why can't someone else do it?"

"Anyone else would fumble it. Anyone else would foul it up. Senator Libby fouled it up once, disastrously, years ago. Rinehart's lived for a hundred and nineteen years, and he's been learning new tricks every year. I've only lived fifty-six years so far, but I'm onto his tricks. I can beat him."

"But why *you?*"

"Somebody's got to do it. My card is on top."

On the desk a telephone buzzed. Dr. Moss answered, then handed Dan the receiver. A moment later the senator was grinning like a cat, struggling into his overcoat and scarf. "Sorry, Doc. I know what you tell me is true, and I'm no fool. If I really have to stop, I'll stop."

"Tomorrow, then."

"Not tomorrow. One of my lads is back from Ironstone Colony with the key to the whole thing in his head. We've got hard work to do tomorrow, but I think I can get the Hearings rescheduled a bit sooner, say next week. When they're over with, I'll be in, scout's honor. Meanwhile, keep your eye on the TV. I'll be seeing you, lad."

The door clicked shut behind him, leaving a faint blue cloud of cigar smoke in his wake. Dr. David Moss stared at it gloomily. "I hope so," he said softly to himself, "I truly hope so."

3

A WHITE Volta two-wheeler was waiting for him outside. Jean Fowler drove off with characteristic contempt for the laws of gravity after her father had piled in. Carl Golden was there, looking thinner, more gaunt and hawklike than ever before, his brown eyes sharp under his shock of black hair. Dan clapped him on the shoulder, and shot a dark look at his daughter, relegating her to some private Fowler limbo, which was where she belonged and would remain until Dan got excited about something and forgot how she'd betrayed her ailing father to Dr. Moss, a matter of fifteen minutes at the most. Jean Fowler knew her father far too well to worry about it. She squinted out the window at the afternoon traffic as the car squealed around the cloverleaf onto the Boulevard Freeway, its stabilizing gyros whining, and then buzzed across the river toward town. "Confound it, boy," Dan was saying, "you could at least have flashed a signal that you were coming. Jean spotted you on the passenger list, and I had to do black-flips to get old MacKenzie to reschedule the Hearings for next week instead of two months from now."

Carl scowled. "I thought the dates were all set."

Dan chuckled. "They were. But it was you we had to wait

for, and with you back with the true story on Armstrong why delay?" He didn't mention the doctor's urgent warning.

Carl Golden shook his head. "I don't like the switch in dates, Dan."

"Well, Dwight MacKenzie didn't like it either, but he's still setting the committee's business calendar, and he couldn't find a good solid reason why the Hearings *shouldn't* be rescheduled. And I think our good friend Senator Rinehart is probably wriggling on the stick right now, just on the shock value of the switch. Always figure in the shock value of everything you do, my boy; it pays off more than you'd ever dream."

"I still don't like it. I wish you hadn't done it."

"But why? Look, lad, I know that with Ken Armstrong dead we had to change our whole approach. It's going to be trickier, without him, but it might even work out better. The Senate knows what's been going on between Rinehart and me. So does the President. They know elections are coming up next June. They know I want a seat on the Criterion Committee before elections, and they know that to get a seat I've got to unseat Rinehart. They know I've shaken him up, that he's scared of me. Okay, fine. With Armstrong here to tell how and why he was chosen for Retread back in '87, what he had to pay Rinehart to get the nod, we'd have had Rinehart running for his life—"

"But you don't have Armstrong here," Carl cut in flatly, "and that's that."

"No, I don't, but believe me, before I get through with him, Rinehart's going to wish I did. *I needed Armstrong badly.* Rinehart knew that, and had him taken care of. It was fishy, it stank from here to Mars, but Rinehart covered it up fast and clean. Well, it was wasted effort. With the stuff you got from the Ironstone Colony files we can charge Rinehart with murder, and the whole Senate knows his motive already. He didn't *dare* let Armstrong testify."

Carl was shaking his head sadly.

"Well, what's wrong?"

"You aren't going to like this, Dan, but I'm afraid Rinehart had nothing to do with Kenneth Armstrong's death."

Fowler gaped at him. "Nothing to *do* with it!"

"Nothing. Armstrong committed suicide."

Dan Fowler sat back hard. "Oh, no."

"Sorry."

"Ken Armstrong? *Suicided?*" Dan shook his head helplessly, groping for words. "I—I—oh, Carl, you've *got* to be wrong. I *knew* Ken Armstrong."

"No, I'm not wrong. There are plenty of things that are very strange about that Mars colony, but Armstrong's death was suicide. Period. Even Barness couldn't believe it at the time and still doesn't know why."

Sharp eyes went to Carl's face. "What's so 'very strange' about the colony?"

Carl Golden shrugged. "Hard to put a finger on it. This was my first look at Ironstone, I had nothing to compare it with. But there's *something* wrong out there. I always thought the Mars colony was a frontier, a real challenge—you know, Man against the Wilderness, and all that. Hard men, hard work, saloons jammed on Saturday night, the sort of place that could take Earthbound softies and toughen them up in two weeks, working to tame the desert—" his voice trailed off. "Well, there's not much hard work going on, that I could see, and when a good man goes up there he just gets softer, not tougher. They've got a saloon, all right, but everybody just goes in there to get drunk and wish that something, somehow, sometime would *happen*. I met a guy named Fisher, must have been a top rate man when he went out there, five years ago. A real go-getter, leader type, lots of ideas and the guts to put them across. Now he's got a hobnail liver and a very warm friendship with port wine and not much else. He came back home on the ship with me, hating Mars and everything up there, most of all himself. Something's gone wrong up there, Dan. Maybe that's why Armstrong took the route he did."

The senator took a deep breath. "Not a man like Ken Armstrong. I used to worship him when I was a kid. You know, I was just ten years old when he came back to Earth for his second Retread." He shook his head. "I wanted to go back to Mars with him. I actually packed up to run away, until dear brother Paul caught me and squealed to Dad. Imagine."

"I'm sorry, Dan."

The car whizzed off the freeway and began weaving through the residential areas of Arlington. Jean swung under an arched gate, stopped in front of a large greystone house of the sort they hadn't built for a hundred years. Dan Fowler stared out at the grey November afternoon. "Well, then we're *really* on thin ice at the Hearings. Nothing really solid at all. If I can't *prove* that Rinehart has corrupted his job, we're in trouble. Well, we've slugged out some tough ones before, and won. This may take some steamrollering, but we can manage it." He turned to the girl. "I'll have to go over Carl's report for anything I can find in it first. Meanwhile, get Dr. Schirmer on the line. Tell him I said if he wants his job as Chief Coordinator of the Hoffman Medical Center next year, he'd better have all the statistics there are on all rejuvenated persons, past and present, in my office by tomorrow morning at eight."

Jean Fowler avoided her father's eyes. "Dr. Schirmer's waiting for you inside right now. He's been here over an hour."

"Here? What for?"

"He wouldn't say. Nothing to do with politics, he said. Something about Uncle Paul."

4

DR. NATHAN SCHIRMER, chubby and nervous, was waiting in the library, sipping a brandy and pretending without success to appear interested in a Congressional Record on the tape-reader. He looked up, birdlike, as Dan Fowler strode in. Dan shook his hand like an old friend. "Good to see you, Nathan. Sit down, sit down. Wanted to chew the fat with you anyway, but what's this about my brother?"

The doctor coughed into his hand. "Why—nothing, really. I mean nothing urgent. I just thought you'd want to know that Paul was in Washington this afternoon."

"Of course he was. He was scheduled to go to the center—" Dan broke off short, whirling on Schirmer. "Wait a minute! There wasn't a slip-up on his permit somehow?"

Dr. Schirmer looked blank. "Permit?"

"For rejuvenation, you idiot! He's on the Starship Project, coordinating engineer of the whole works out there. He's got a fair place on the list coming to him three ways from Sunday. MacKenzie put the permit through months ago, and Paul has just been fooling around clearing the decks out in Vegas so he could come in—"

The coordinator's eyes widened. "Oh, there wasn't anything wrong on *our* side if that's what you mean. The permit was in perfect order, the doctors at the center were ready and waiting for him. *That* isn't the trouble."

"Then what is?"

The doctor flushed. "Well, I'll be blunt. The trouble is, your brother refused. He flew all the way out here, right on schedule, just to laugh in our faces and tell us to go fly a kite. Then he got on the next jet back to Nevada. All in one afternoon."

5

THE VIBRATION of the jet engines hung just at perception level, nagging and nagging at Dan Fowler, until he threw his papers aside with a snarl of disgust and peered angrily out the window at nothing.

The plane was high and moving fast. Far below was a tiny spot of light in the blackness. Pittsburgh, maybe, or Cleveland. Didn't matter which. Jets went at such-and-such a speed; they left one place at such-and-such a time and arrived somewhere else so many hours or minutes later, and worrying didn't move them any faster. He could worry, or not worry, it was all the same; he would be in Las Vegas at exactly the same time, to the second, either way. Then another half-hour taxi ride over dusty desert roads would bring him to the glorified Quonset hut his brother called home. And now Dan Fowler, that crafty old specialist in the art of getting the immovable to move when he wanted it to move, could not speed by one iota the process of getting there.

Dan had tried to call Paul from Washington, and received no answer. He had talked to the Las Vegas authorities, and to Starship Project Headquarters; he'd even talked to Lijinsky, who was running Starship, but nobody knew anything. The police said yes, they would check at Dr. Fowler's residence, if he wasn't out at the ship, and then call right back, but they hadn't called back, and that was two hours ago. Meanwhile, Carl had chartered Dan a plane.

Now, staring out at the blackness, Dan clenched his fist, drove it into his palm again and again. Ten thousand devils take Paul! Of all miserable times for him to start playing games, acting like an idiot child! And the work and sweat Dan had gone through to get that permit for him, to buy it, beg it, steal it, gold-plate it. Of course the odds were good that Paul would have gotten it anyway without so much as a nod from Dan—he was high on the committee's priority list, a key man on the Starship Project, which certainly rated top national priority. But with Rinehart heading the committee, Dan couldn't take a chance. He'd personally gone out on a limb, way out—the senator clenched his teeth in helpless frustration and anger, and felt a twinge of pain blossom in his chest, spread to his shoulder and arm. He cursed, fumbled for the bottle in his vest pocket. Confounded heart and confounded brother and confounded Rinehart—why did *everything* have to break the wrong way *now?* Of all the times in his fifty-six years of life, why *now?*

All right, Dan. Cool off, boy. Relax. Shame on you. Why not quit being selfish just for a minute? Dan didn't like the idea as it flickered through his mind, but then he didn't like anything too much right then, so he hauled the thought back for a rerun. Big Dan Fowler, *Senator* Dan Fowler, Selfish Dan Fowler loves Dan Fowler, mostly.

Poor Paul.

The words had been pounding in his mind like words in an echo-chamber ever since he had seen Dr. Schirmer and heard what he had to say. Poor Paul. Brother Dan did all right for himself, he did; made quite a name for himself down in Washington, you know, a fighter, a real fighter. The Boy with the Golden Touch (mocking laughter from the wings). Everything he ever did worked out with him on top, somehow. Not Paul, though. Paul was different. Smart enough, plenty going for him, but he never had Dan's drive, Dan's persuasiveness, Dan's ruthlessness. Nothing but bad breaks for brother Paul, right down the line. Kinda tough on a guy, with a fireball like Dan in the family. Poor Paul.

Dan let his mind drift back, slowly, remembering little things, trying to pin down just when it was, what single instant in time, that he had stopped fighting Paul and started pitying him. It had been different, years before. Paul was always the smart one, then. He never had Dan's build, or Dan's daring, but he could think rings around him. Dan was always a little slow—never forgot anything he learned, but he was a slow study. Until he found out there were ways to get around that. Dad and Mom had always favored Paul, babied him and protected him, and that was tougher to get around, but there were ways.

There was the night the prize money came from the lottery. How old was he then? Twelve? Thirteen? Paul was seventeen. Dan had grubbed up ten dollars polishing cars, and matched Paul's ten to split a ticket down the middle. Never dreamed the thing would pay off, the National Tax Lottery was very new at that time. And then, to their stunned amazement, it *did* pay off, two thousand dollars cash, quite a pile for a pair of boys. Enough to buy the jet racer Dan had his heart set on. He'd been so excited tears had poured down his face, but Paul had said no. They would split the money fifty-fifty, just like the ticket, Paul had said. There were hot words, and pleading, and threats, and Paul had just laughed at him, until Dan got so mad he sailed into him with his fists. Bad mistake, that. Paul was skinny, not much muscle, but he had five years on Dan, and a longer reach. Paul connected just once, a left jab that put Dan flat on his back with a concussion and a broken jaw, and that was that.

Or so it seemed, except that Dan had actually won the fight the moment Paul struck the blow. It was the broken jaw that did it, and then later the fight between Mom and Dad, with Dad saying, "But Mary, he *asked* for it!" And Mom responding tearfully, "I don't care, that big bully didn't have to *mutilate* him." Of course Dan won. A dirty way to win, both the boys knew, but Dan got his racer on the strength of that broken jaw. The bone never healed quite right, the fracture damaged one of the centers of ossification, the doc had said, and later Dan became God's gift to the political cartoonists with that heavy, angular jaw—a fighter's jaw, they called it.

That fight started it. From then on Dan knew he could beat Paul. He didn't feel good about the way he'd beaten him, but it was a good thing to know he could. Couldn't ever be *sure* of it, of course, had to keep proving it, over and over, just to be sure. The successes came, and he always let Paul know about them, chuckling with glee, while Paul sat quietly, learning to take it.

To take it? Or to fight back, ineffectually, and slowly come to hate him? Hard to say. There was the night Dan broke with the Universalist Party in New Chicago, at that hundred-dollar-a-plate dinner. He'd told them all, that night. The big boys in the party had cold-shouldered him and put Jack Libby up to run for mayor instead of Dan. Oh, he'd raised a glorious stink that night—he'd never enjoyed himself so much in his life, turning their whole lousy twisted machine over to the public on a silver platter. Cutting loose from the old crowd, appointing himself a committee of one to nominate himself on an Independent Reform ticket, campaign for himself, and elect himself. A whippersnapper of thirty-two. Paul had laughed at the blistering speech he'd given before he stomped out of the banquet hall. "You *do* get melodramatic, don't you, Dan? Well, if you want to cut your own throat, that's your affair." Dan had exploded in rage, told Paul to watch what happened before he shot off his mouth, he might see a thing or two—and he saw a thing or two, all right. He remembered Paul's face a few months later, when Libby conceded his defeat at 11:45 on election night, and Dan rode into office with a new crowd of people ready to help him clean up New Chicago as it hadn't been cleaned up since the Two Weeks' War. The sweetest bite of the whole victory pie had been the look on Paul's face that night.

So they'd fought, and Dan had won and rubbed it in, and Paul had lost and hated him for it, until slowly, Dan's attitude had subtly changed from "Okay, you wise guy, I'll show you" to "Come *on,* Paul, quit floundering around and start *doing* something! Who needs engineers? You'll starve to death," and then finally, to "Poor Paul."

How had it happened? Why?

Dan wondered, suddenly, if he had ever really forgiven Paul that blow to the jaw.

Perhaps.

He shook himself, scowling into the blackness outside the plane. Okay, they'd fought it out, a game between brothers, only it never was a game, really. He knew how much he owed to Paul. He'd known it with growing concern for many years. And now if he had to drag Paul back to Washington by the hair, he'd drag the silly fool.

6

THEY DIDN'T look very much alike. There was a spareness about Paul, a tall, lean man, with large soft eyes that concealed their anger and a face lined with tiredness and resignation. A year ago, when Dan had seen him last, he had looked a young sixty, closer to forty-five. Now he looked an old, old sixty-one. How much of this was his illness Dan didn't know. The pathologist at the Hoffman Center had said: "It's not very malignant right now, but you can never tell when it'll blow up, and it's one of the new viral tumors that we can't deal with just yet. He'd better be scheduled for his Retread as soon as possible, if he's got a permit."

That was doubtless part of it, but part of it was just Paul.

The house was exactly as Dan had expected (though he had never been inside this house since Paul had come to Starship Project fifteen years ago), stuffy, severe, rather gloomy; rooms packed with bookshelves, drawing boards, odds and ends of papers and blueprints and inks; thick, ugly furniture from the early 2000's; a cluttered, improvised, helter-skelter barn of a testing lab, with modern equipment that looked lost and alien scattered among the mouldering junk of two centuries.

"Get your coat," said Dan to his brother. "It's cold outside. We're going back to Washington."

"Have a drink." Paul waved him toward the sideboard. "Relax. Your pilot needs a rest."

"Paul, I didn't come here to play games. The games are over now."

Paul poured brandy with deliberation, one for Dan, one for himself. "Good brandy," he said. "Wish I could afford more of it."

"*Paul*. You're going with me."

"Sorry, Dan."

"Do you know what you're saying?"

"Perfectly."

"Paul, you don't just say 'Thanks, but I don't think I'll have any' when they give you a rejuvenation permit. *Nobody* refuses rejuvenation. There are a million people out there begging for a place on the list. It's *life*, Paul. You can't just turn it down."

"This *is* good brandy," said Paul. "Care to take a look at my lab, by the way? Not too well equipped, but sometimes I can work here better than—"

Dan turned on his brother viciously. "I will tell you what I'm going to do," he said, hitting each syllable. "I'm going to take you to the plane. If you won't come, my pilot and I will drag you. When we get to Washington, we'll take you to the Hoffman Center. If you won't sign the necessary releases, I'll forge them. I'll bribe two witnesses who will swear in the face of death by torture that they saw you signing. I'll buy the doctors that can do the job, and if they don't do it, I'll sweat them down until they *will* do it."

He slammed the glass down on the table, heart pounding in his throat, pain creeping up his chest. "I've got lots of things on lots of people, and I can get things done when I want them done. People don't fool with me in Washington any more, because when they do they get their fingers burned off at the knuckles. Paul, I knew you were stubborn but I didn't think you were blockheaded stupid!"

Paul shrugged.

"You don't think I could do it?" Dan roared.

"Oh, I suppose you *could*. But it's a lot of trouble for such an unwilling victim. And I'm your brother, Dan. Remember?"

Dan Fowler spread his hands in defeat, sank down in the chair. "Paul, tell me *why*."

"I don't want to be rejuvenated." As though he were saying, "I don't want any sugar in my coffee."

"Why not? If I could only see why, if I knew what was going through your mind, maybe I could understand. But I can't." Dan looked up at Paul, pleading. "You're *needed,* Paul. I had a tape from Lijinsky last month. Do you know what he said? He said he wished you'd come to Starship ten years sooner. Nobody knows that ship the way you do, you're making it go. That ship can take men to the stars, now, with rejuvenation, and the same men can come back again to find the same people waiting for them when they get here. They can *live* that long, now. We've been tied down to seventy years of life, to a tight little universe of one sun and nine planets for thousands of years. Well, we can change that now. We can go out. That's what your work can do for us." He stared helplessly at his brother. "You could go out on that ship you're building, Paul. You've always wanted to. *Why not?*"

Paul looked across at him for a long moment. There was pity in his eyes. There was also bitterness there, and victory, long awaited, painfully won. "Do you really want me to tell you?"

"I want you to tell me."

Then Paul told him. It took about ten minutes. It was not tempered with mercy.

It split Dan Fowler's world wide open at the seams.

"You've been talking about the Starship," said Paul Fowler. "All right, that's a good place to start. I came to Starship Project, what was it, fifteen years ago? Sixteen, I guess. This was my meat. I didn't work well with people, I worked with *things*, processes, ideas. I dug in hard on Starship. I loved it, dreamed it, lived with it. I had dreams in those days. Work hard, make myself invaluable here, maybe *I'd* get rejuvenation, so that I could go on working. I believed everything you just said then. Alpha Centauri, Arcturus, Vega, anywhere we wanted to go, and I could go along! It wouldn't be long, either. We had Lijinsky back with us after his rejuvenation, directing the project, we had Keller and Stark and Eddie Cochran—great men, the men who had pounded Starship Project into reality, took it out of the storybooks and made the people of this country want it badly enough to pay for it. Those men were back now, new men, rebuilt bodies, with all their knowledge and experience preserved. Only now they had something even more precious than life: *time*. And I was part of it, and I too could have time."

Paul shook his head, slowly, and sank back into the chair. His eyes were very tired. "A dream, nothing more. A fantasy. It took me fifteen years to learn what a dream it was. Nothing at first, just a vague puzzlement, things happening that I couldn't quite grasp. Easy to shrug off, until it got too obvious. Not a matter of wrong decisions, really. The decisions were right, but they were in the wrong places. Something about Starship Project shifting, changing somehow. Something being lost. Slowly. Nothing you could nail down, at first, but growing month by month.

"Then one night I saw what it was. That was when I equipped the lab here, and proved to myself that Starship Project was a dream."

He spread his hands and smiled at Dan like a benign old schoolmaster at a third-grade schoolboy. "That starship isn't going to Alpha Centauri or anywhere else. It's never going to leave the ground. I thought I'd live long enough to launch that ship and be one of its crew. Well, I won't. That ship wouldn't leave the ground if I lived a million years."

"Rubbish," said Dan Fowler succinctly.

"No, Dan. Not rubbish. Unfortunately, sometimes we have to quit dreaming and look facts in the face. Starship Project is dying. Our whole society is dying. Nimrock drove the first nail into the coffin a hundred and thirty years ago. Oh, if they'd only hanged him when his first rejuvenation attempt failed! But that would only have delayed it. We're dying slowly right now, but soon it will be fast, very fast. And do you know the man who is getting ready to deal us our death blow?" He smiled sadly across at his brother. "You are, Dan."

Dan Fowler sprang from his chair with a roar. "Paul, you're *sick!* Of all the idiotic remarks I ever heard, I— I— oh, Paul." He stood shaking, groping for words, staring at his brother.

"You said you wanted me to tell you."

"Tell me what?" Dan took a trembling breath, and sat down, visibly fighting for control. "All right, all right, I heard what you said. You must mean something, but I don't know what. Let's be reasonable. Let's forget philosophy and semantics and concepts and all the frills for just a minute and talk about facts, huh? *Just facts.*"

"All right, facts," said Paul. "Kenneth Armstrong wrote *Man on Mars* in 2028. He was fifty-seven years old then, and he hadn't been rejuvenated yet. Fundamentally a good book, analyzing his first Mars colony, taking it apart right down to the ground, studies to show why it had failed so miserably, and why the next one could succeed if he could ever get up there again. He had foresight; with rejuvenation just getting started, he had a whole flock of ideas about overpopulation and the need for a Mars colony. He was all wet on the population angle, of course, but nobody knew that then. He got Keller and Lijinsky all excited with the Starship idea. They admit it— it was *Man on Mars* that first started them thinking. They were both young then, with lots of fight in them—"

"Just stick to facts," said Dan coldly.

"Okay. Starship Project got started, and blossomed into the people's baby. They started work on the basic blueprints about sixty years ago. Everybody knew it would be a long job, costly, very costly, with so much to do before the building even began, but that was all right. The planning took over forty years, and that was where I came in, fifteen years ago. Building the ship. They were looking for engineers who weren't eager to get rich. It went fine. We started to build. Then Keller and Stark came back from rejuvenation. Lijinsky had been rejuvenated five years before."

"Look, I don't need a course in history," Dan exploded.

"Yes, you do," Paul snapped. "You need to sit down and listen for once, instead of just shooting off your big mouth." Paul Fowler rubbed his chin. "Okay, there were some changes made. I didn't like the engine housing, I never had, so I went along with them a hundred percent on that. I was the one who had designed it, but even I had learned a few things since. And there were bugs. It made good sense, when you talked to Lijinsky. Starship Project was pretty important to all of us. Dangerous to risk a fumble on the first play, even a tiny risk. We might never get another chance. Lijinsky knew we youngsters were driving along on adrenalin and nerves, and couldn't wait to get out there, but when you thought about it, what was the rush? Why risk a failure just to get out there *this* year instead of *next?* Couldn't we take time to find a valid test for that engine at ultra-high acceleration before we put it back in? After all, we *had* time now—Keller and Stark just back with sixty more years to live—why the rush?

"Okay, I bought it. We worked out a valid test chamber on paper. Took four years to find out we couldn't build such a device on Earth, but never mind that. Other things were getting stalled in the meantime. The colony plan for the ship —was it the best possible? Choosing the crew—what criteria, what qualifications? There was plenty of time—why not make *sure* it's right? Don't leave anything crude, if we can refine it a little first."

Paul sighed wearily. "It snowballed. Keller and Stark backed Lijinsky to the hilt. There was trouble about money—I think you had your thumb in the pie there, getting it fixed for us, didn't you? More refinement. Work it out. Details. Get side-tracked on some aspect for a few years, so what? Lots of time. Rejuvenation, and all that, talk about the Universalists beating Rinehart out and throwing the center open to everybody. And so on, and so on. And somewhere along the line I began to see that it just wasn't true. The holdups, the changes, the digressions and snags and refinements were all excuses, all part of a big, beautiful, exquisitely reasonable facade that was completely obscuring the real truth. *Lijinsky and Keller and Stark had changed.*"

Dan Fowler snorted. "I know a very smart young doctor who told me that there *aren't* any changes with rejuvenation."

"Nothing physical, their bodies were fine. Nothing mental, either, they had the same sharp minds they always had. Just a subtle change in values. They'd lost something they'd had before. The *drive* that made them start Starship Project, the *urgency,* the vital importance of the thing—all gone. They didn't have the push they once had. They began looking for the slow, easy way, and it was far easier to build and rebuild, and refine, and improve the Starship here on the ground than to throw that Starship out into space."

There was a long, long silence. Dan Fowler sat grey-faced, staring at Paul, just shaking his head and staring. "I don't believe it," he said finally. "I've seen Lijinsky's reports. There's been progress, regular progress, month by month. You've been too close to it, maybe. Of course there have been delays, but only when they were necessary. The progress has gone on—"

"No, not so," Paul said. He stood up, pulled out drawers, dragged out rolls of blueprints. "These are my own. They're based on the working prints from Starship that we drew up ten years ago, scaled down to model size. I've tested them, I've run tolerances, I've checked the math five ways and back again. I've tested the parts, the engine—model size. There is no flaw in these blueprints. They're as perfect as they'll ever get."

Anger was blazing in Paul's voice now, bitterness and frustration. "I could built this model and send it out to Alpha Centauri next week, and *it would get there*. The Starship Project is completed, it's been completed for ten years now, but do you know what happened to these blueprints, the originals? They were studied, and thrown out in favor of refinements and modifications—"

"But I've read the reports," Dan cried.

"Have you seen the *Starship*?"

"Well—no."

"I didn't think you had. You haven't actually *talked* with Lijinsky and the other Retreads heading up the project, either. Well, it isn't just here, Dan. It's everywhere. There are only about 70,000 rejuvenated men alive in this hemisphere so far, but already the change is beginning to show. Go talk to the

advertising people; there's a delicate indicator of social change
if there ever was one. See what *they* say. Whose policy on
rejuvenation are *they* backing up in the government? Yours?
Don't kid yourself. They aren't even backing Walter Rinehart.
They're backing 'Moses' Tyndall and his Abolitionist goon-
squad, the crowd who go around preaching that rejuvenation
is the work of the Devil. And they've given Tyndall enough of
a push that he's even getting *you* worried now. Then how about
Roderigo Aviado and his Solar Energy Project down in Antarctica? Do you know what *he's* been doing lately? You ought
to find out, Dan. What's going on in the Mars colony? You
ought to find out. Have you gone to talk to any of the Noble
Ten who are still rattling around? You ought to, you might get
quite a jolt. And how about all the suicides in the last ten
years? What do the insurance people say about that?"

Paul stopped, from lack of breath. Dan just stared at him.
"Find out what you're *doing*, Dan, before you push this universal rejuvenation idea of yours through. We've had a monster
on our hands for years now without even knowing it. And now
Big Dan Fowler has to play God and turn the thing loose on
the world. Well, look before you plunge in. It's all here, if
you'd just open your eyes to see it, but you're so dead certain
that you want life everlasting that you've never even bothered
to *look*. Nobody's bothered to look. And now it's such a grand
political bludgeon that nobody *dares* to look."

Dan Fowler rose, walked over to the blueprints, ran his
finger over the dusty paper. His face was old when he turned
back to Paul. "You've believed all this for a long time, haven't
you?" he said.

"A long time," said Paul.

"All the time I've been working like a dog to build up support for my universal rejuvenation program."

Paul's eyes flickered. "That's right."

"And you never said one word to me." Dan shook his head

slowly. "I didn't know you hated me so much. But I'm not going to let you win this one, either, Paul. You're wrong. And I'm going to prove that you're wrong if it kills me."

7

"THEN try his home number," Dan Fowler snarled into the booth telephone. He gnawed his cigar and fumed as long seconds spun by on the wall clock, then minutes. His fingers drummed the wall. "How's that? Confound it, I want to speak to Dwight MacKenzie himself, not some flunky. What do you mean, he's not in town? I saw him with my own eyes yesterday."

Another wait, five minutes this time, then another voice, with profuse apologies but no Dwight MacKenzie. "All right, then track him down for me and have him call me back." He reeled off the number of his private booth.

Carl Golden looked up as Dan came back to the cafeteria table and stirred up his half-cold coffee. "No luck?"

"Seems that MacKenzie has vanished. Convenient, eh?" Dan leaned back against the wall, glowering at Carl and Jean. Through the transparent walls of the glassed-in booth, they could see the morning breakfast-seekers drifting into the place. "Well, you were surely right, lad. I should never have tampered with those Hearing dates in the first place. But Dwight will switch them back again to give us the time we need. MacKenzie is no ball of fire, but he's always backed me up. We should hear from him pretty soon." He bit off the end of a fresh cigar, assaulted it with a match.

"Dad, you know what Dr. Moss said—"

"Look, little girl, you'd better lay off," Dan snapped. "I've got enough worries without having Dr. Moss on my back as well." He sipped his coffee while both the young people picked at their breakfast with bleary early-morning resignation. Carl Golden needed a shave badly.

"Did you get any sleep on the way back?" he asked Dan.

Dan snorted. "What do you think?"

"I think Paul might be lying to you."

Dan shot him a sharp glance. "Maybe, but I doubt it. Paul has always been fussy about the truth. He's all wrong, of course —" (fresh coffee, not much hotter than the last)—" but I think *he* believes his tale."

"Well, if he really believes it, I don't like it. There's too much of what he said that rings a bell somewhere."

Dan clanked the cup down and swore. "He's demented, that's what he is! He's waited too long for his Retread, and his brain's starting to go. If his idea were true, why did he wait so long to tell somebody about it?"

"Maybe he wanted to see you hang yourself."

"But I can only hang myself on *facts*, not on the paranoid delusions of a sick old man. No, Paul is wrong—he's got to be wrong." Dan broke off, staring across at Carl. "Look, boy, if he *isn't* wrong, then we're whipped, that's all. And I've spent thirty years of my life perpetrating some kind of hideous fraud on the people of this country."

"But you can't blame yourself if you didn't *know*," Jean Fowler protested.

"That's what you think, kiddie. I'm not a meek, harmless little mouse like Dwight MacKenzie. I've got the loudest mouth in the Senate. I scream and shout and knock heads together and get things done, and when a man does it that way it's his *job* to know what he's doing. Well, now I *don't* know. I think Paul's wrong, but do you think *I'd* care to walk into the Hoffman Center for a Retread right now without being sure? Not on your life. Any more than I could walk into those Hearings next week. We've got to stop everything and find out, right now and for certain, whether Paul's wrong or not."

He dragged a sheaf of yellow paper out of his pocket and spread it on the table. "I worked out a plan on the way back. We've got a tough job on our hands, more than we can possibly handle before next week. So number one job is to shift the Hearings back again. I'll take care of that as soon as I can get MacKenzie on the wire."

"What are you giving him for a reason?" Jean wanted to know.

"Anything but the truth. Doesn't matter. MacKenzie is convinced I'm going to win at the Hearings, and he wants to be on the right side of the toast when it's buttered. He'll shove the date back to February 15. Okay, next we need a crew—a crowd of people who can do fast, accurate, hard work and not squeal if they don't sleep for a month or so. Bob Sandborn is in Washington, he can handle statistics for us. Jack Torrelli has good contacts with the insurance people. In addition, we need a couple of good sharp detectives. Any ideas, Jean?"

"A couple. I'll need time to reach them, though."

"How much time?"

"A day or two."

"Then get on it. We'll have lots for them to do by tomorrow." The senator turned back to Carl. "I want you to hit Starship Project first."

Carl shook his head. "Not me, there's a better man for the job. Saw him last night, and he's dying for something to do. Terry Fisher. He'll know how to dig out what we want. He was doing it on Mars for five years."

Dan frowned. "He was also on the bottle, Carl. We can't take a risk like that."

"There won't be any risk. Terry drank to get away from what he found on Mars, that's all. He's not drinking now."

"Well, if you say so. I'll want to see the Starship setup, too, but I want it ready for a quick scan. Get hold of Fisher this morning and get him clearance papers for Nevada. You'd better tackle the ad men yourself then, while Torrelli hits Metro Insurance. Don't waste time with underlings, go to the top and wave my name around like a flag. They won't like it a bit, but they know I've got a string on Kornwall in Communications. We'll have his scalp if they don't play ball with us. All you have to do is make sure that they believe it."

"What's on Kornwall?"

"Kornwall has been fronting for 'Moses' Tyndall for years. That's why Tyndall never bothered me too much, because I could have gotten him through Kornwall any time I wanted to. And the ad-men and Metro have everything they own sunk into Tyndall's political plans."

"I see," Carl said, but his frown lingered. "If you're sure."

"Of course I'm sure. Don't worry about it, lad. It's okay."

"I just hope you're not underestimating John Tyndall."

"Why?"

"I used to work for him, remember? And he doesn't like you. He knows in the long run it's going to be you or he, one or the other, who rides this rejuvenation issue right into the White House. Well, what happens if 'Moses' gets wind of this mess? Say that he finds out what your brother told you, or even finds out that you're worried about something?"

Dan chewed his lip. "He *could* be a pain, all right."

"He sure could. More than just a pain, and Kornwall wouldn't be much help, either, if the news got out."

"Well, it's a risk we have to take, that's all. We'll have to be fast and quiet." Dan Fowler pushed his coffee cup aside and jumped for the phone booth when the blinker began flashing. "This will get us started, at least. Jean, you keep somebody on the switchboard, and keep track of us all. When I get through with MacKenzie, I may be out of touch for a day or so. You'll have to be my ears, and cover for me." And to the phone: "*Yes*, yes. I was calling Dwight MacKenzie——" Pause. "Hello, Dwight?—What? Well, balls of fire! *Where is he?* Timagami— *Ontario?* An island!" He covered the speaker and looked at Carl. "He's gone moosehunting." Then: "Okay, so there isn't any phone. Get me Eastern Sea-Jet Charter Service instead."

Twenty minutes later Dan Fowler was in the air again, flying north into an evil-looking winter sky.

8

A LONG SERIES of grey, flickering pictures, then, for Dan Fowler. A fast sandwich eaten on the plane as the Capitol's pale sun was swallowed up. A grey sky, then almost black, temperature dropping, a grey drizzling rain. Cold. Wind bouncing the grey shape of the little ski-plane around like a stick in a stream. Grey news from the pilot: "Eight feet of snow up there, according to reports. Lake's frozen three feet thick. Going to be a rough ride, Senator." A grey memory of Jean's quick kiss before he climbed aboard, the sharp worry in her eyes—"Got your pills, Dad? Try to sleep. Take it easy. Give me a call about anything——" (Tough thing to do without any phones, but why tell her that? She's already scared enough. Confounded heart, anyway). A wobbly takeoff that almost dumped his stomach into his lap and sent the briefcase flying across the cabin. Then rain, and grey-black nothing out there as they headed north. Faster, man, can't you get this crate to *move* a little? Sorry, Senator, nasty currents up here. Maybe if we go higher—

Time! Paul had said it was more precious than life, and

now time ran screaming by in great deadly sweeps, like a black-winged buzzard. And through it all, weariness, tiredness that Dan had never felt before. Not the weariness of years, nor of hard work, just a grey, heartsick sense that time at last was running out on him. He should have rejuvenated months ago, then at least he'd have time. But now—*what if Paul were right?*

No rejuvenation for Dan Fowler now, of course. Not until Paul is proven wrong, a thousand times wrong. That was it, that was the real weariness that wasn't time-weariness or body-weariness. Just mind-weariness. Weariness at the thought of wasted work, the wasted years—a wasted life. Unless Paul were proven wrong.

Angry at his greyness, Dan snapped on the little TV, searched for diversion. Wonderful pickup these days. News of the world brought to you by Atomics International, the fuel that will power the Starship . . . the President returned to Washington today after three-week vacation conference in Calcutta with Chinese and Indian dignitaries . . . full accord and a cordial ending to the meeting . . . American medical supplies to be made available . . . and on the home front, appropriations renewed for Antarctica Project . . . solar energy in every home within a decade, according to Project Director Roderigo Aviado. . . . Special bulletin: huge Abolitionist rally last night in New Chicago as John 'Moses' Tyndall returned to that city for the fifteenth anniversary of the movement he started there back in 2119 . . . cut to scene of wild, placard-waving crowd and a huge banner proclaiming DOWN WITH REJUVENATION THE DEVILS WORK . . . then back to Tyndall's hawk face and strident voice lashing out at Senator Daniel Fowler's universal rejuvenation program . . . twenty-five hour work week hailed by Senator Rinehart of Alaska as a great progressive step for the American people . . . Senator Rinehart, chairman of the all-powerful Criterion Committee, holding forth hope last night that improved rejuvenation techniques may enable the Hoffman Center to handle up to six hundred candidates a year within five years. . . . Dan snarled in disgust, cut Rinehart's comforting, confidence-inspiring face off in mid-smile.

His ears popped and the plane was descending, then, into flurries of northern snow. He peered out at the whiter gloom below, a long stretch of white with blobs of black on either side, resolving into snow-laden black pines, a vast expanse of frozen, snow-covered lake, the slight jolt as the skis touched down. Taxiing across a cove of the lake, engines roaring, throwing up a whirlwind of powdery snow. And ahead, on the shore above the lake, a black blot of a house, with yellow window lights glowing warm and cheerful in the middle of this frozen wilderness.

Then Dwight MacKenzie, mouselike, peering out into the gloom, startled eyes with streaks of fear in them, widening in recognition. MacKenzie throwing open the door, smiling, pumping Dan's hand, a too-hearty greeting. "Dan! I couldn't *imagine* who was coming in this snowstorm, hardly ever see anybody up here, you know. Come in, come in, you must be half frozen. What's happened? Something torn loose down in Washington?" And more talk, more questions, tumbling over each other, but something wrong in the voice, no answers wanted, just talk to cover up surprise and fear and the one *real* question of why Dan Fowler should be dropping down out of the winter sky right then.

A huge lodge room, open beams, blazing fire in a mammoth fireplace at the one end, moose heads, a thick black bearhide on the floor. "I like to come up here a day or two before the others arrive for hunting," MacKenzie was saying. "Does a man good to commune with his soul once in a while, eh? You a hunter, Dan? You ought to join us. Libby and Donaldson will be up tomorrow with a couple of guides. There's always an extra rifle around. Ought to be good hunting this year."

One chair near the fireplace, a book hastily thrown down beside it, *Sextra Special*, Cartoons by Kulp. Great book for soul-searching senators. Things were a little out of focus at first after the biting cold, but now Dan was beginning to see. One book, one chair, but two half-filled cocktail glasses at the sideboard—

Dan shook his head. "No thanks, Dwight, I have to get right back to the city. Tried to catch you before you left, nothing too urgent, but I wanted to let you know that I put you to all that trouble for nothing, switching the Hearing dates around. We don't need the Hearings next week after all."

Wariness in MacKenzie's eyes. "Well! It wasn't any trouble, Dan. No trouble at all. Next week was fine with everybody, better than the February date would have been, as a matter of fact. This way the committee can collect itself before Christmas holidays, ha, ha."

"Well, it now seems that it *wouldn't* be so good for me, Dwight. I'd much prefer the dates changed back to February again."

A long silence while MacKenzie pursed his lips. "Well, now. That's—awkward. You know, Dan, we really *have* to settle these things sooner or later. Can't just shove dates around willy-nilly. And to change back at this late date—I just don't know."

"Don't know! Why not? You call the meetings and set the agenda."

The moose-hunter licked his lips. "Yes, but it isn't just me that makes these decisions, Dan. Other people have to be consulted. It's a little late to catch them now, you know. It might be pretty hard to do that."

No more smiles from Dan. "Now look, you make the calendar, and you can change it." Face getting red, getting angry —careful, Dan, those two cocktail glasses, watch what you say —"I want it changed back. And I've got to know right now."

"But you told me you'd be all ready to roll by next week."

No more caution—he *had* to have time. "Look, there's no reason you can't do it if you want to, Dwight. I'd consider it a personal favor—I repeat, a very great personal favor—if you'd make the arrangements. Believe me, I won't forget it." What did the swine want, an arm off at the roots?

"Sorry," said a deep voice from the rear door of the room. Walter Rinehart walked across to the glass on the sideboard. "You don't mind if I finish this, Dwight?"

A deep breath from MacKenzie, like a sigh of relief. "Go right ahead, Walt. Drink, Dan?"

"No, I don't think so." It was Walter, all right. Tall, upright, dignified Walter, fine shock of wavy hair as white as the snow outside. Young-old lines on his face. Some men looked finer after rejuvenation, much finer than before. There had been a weakness in Walter Rinehart's eyes and face before his first Retread. Not now. A fine man, the picture of mature wisdom and social responsibility. A man you could *trust* to guide the committee that decided whether you were going to be the one to live or die.

But inside, the mind was the same as it was before. Inside, no changes. Author of the Rinehart Criteria, back in the days when rejuvenation first became possible. Rinehart's supporters compared that manifesto with the Gettysburg address, with Churchill's "blood, sweat and tears" speech, with the Markheim Doctrine that had finally brought East and West to the end of the Cold War. The criteria to be used by an impartial committee in selecting those individuals most worthy, by service to mankind, to enjoy the fruits of the new rejuvenation process until such time as it could be available to all—Rinehart's work. Some said it was a work of genius, and it secured Walter Rinehart a perpetual seat in the Senate, and chairmanship of the Criterion Committee. But other men, less impressed and more far-seeing—men like Dan Fowler—had insisted that

Rinehart's real intent was to set up a small, self-perpetuating "immortal elite" who would ultimately use their control over rejuvenation as a weapon to control the world.

No one had fought Rinehart harder or longer than Dan Fowler. The world knew that, but the world was not present in this secluded hunting lodge tonight.

Dan turned his back on Rinehart and said to MacKenzie, "I want the date changed."

"I—I can't do it, Dan." An inquiring glance at Rinehart, a faint smiling nod in return.

Suddenly it dawned on Dan how badly he had blundered. MacKenzie was afraid. MacKenzie wanted another lifetime, one of these days. He had decided that Rinehart was the one who could give it to him. But worse, far worse: Rinehart knew now that something had happened, something was wrong. "What's the matter, Dan?" he said smoothly. "You need more time before the Hearings? Why? You had plenty of time before, but you threw it away, made poor Dwight here shift the dates right up under our noses. Now you want them changed back, all of a sudden. What happened, Dan? Hit a snag somewhere?"

That was all. Back against the wall. The thought of bluffing it through, swallowing the December 15 date and telling them to drop dead flashed through his mind. He threw it out violently, his heart sinking. That was only a few days, and he had weeks of work ahead of him. He needed more time, he *had* to have it—

Rinehart was grinning confidently. "Of course I'd like to cooperate, Dan. But I have some plans for the Hearings, too. You've been getting on people's nerves, down in the city. There's even been talk on the committee of revoking your rejuvenation permit."

Your move, Dan. Oh, what a blunder! Why did you ever come up here? And every minute you stand there with your jaw sagging just tells Rinehart how tight he's got you—*do* something, *anything*—

Well, there was a way. Would Carl ever understand it? No telling. Carl had begged him never to use it, ever, under any circumstances, and Carl had trusted him implicitly when he had promised that he wouldn't. It would be an outright betrayal, but if Carl Golden were standing here in his shoes, what would *he* say? He'd say yes, go ahead, use it, wouldn't he? He'd have to.

"I want the Hearings on February 15," Dan said to Rinehart.

"Sorry, Dan. We can't be tossing dates around like that. Unless you care to tell me just why."

"Okay." Dan grabbed his hat angrily. "I'll make a formal request for the change tomorrow morning, and read it on the TV. Then I'll also announce a feature attraction that the people can look forward to when the Hearings begin. We weren't planning to use it, but you seem to want both barrels right in the face, so that's what we'll give you."

Walter Rinehart roared with laughter. "*Another* feature attraction? You do dig them up, don't you? Ken Armstrong's dead, you know."

"Peter Golden's widow isn't."

The smile faded on Rinehart's face. He looked suddenly like a man carved out of grey stone. Dan's whole body was shaking as he let the words sink in. "You didn't think *anybody* knew about that, did you, Walter? That's too bad. We've got the whole story on Peter Golden, the *whole* story. Took quite a while to piece it together, but we did it with the help of his son. Carl remembers his father before the accident, you see, quite well. His widow remembers him even before that. And we have some fascinating video tapes that Peter Golden made when he applied for rejuvenation, and later when he appealed

the committee's decisions. Some of the private interviews, too,
Walter."

"I gave Peter Golden forty more years of life," Rinehart
said.

"You crucified him," said Dan, bluntly.

There was silence, a long silence. Then: "Are you selling?"

"I'm selling." Cut out my tongue, Carl, but I'm selling.

"How do I know you won't use it anyway?"

"You don't know. Except that I'm telling you I won't."

Rinehart soaked that in with the last gulp of his drink.
Then he smashed the glass on the stone floor. "Change the
date," he told MacKenzie. "Then throw this vermin out of
here."

Back in the snow and darkness Dan tried to breathe again,
and couldn't quite make it. He had to stop and rest twice
going down to the plane. Then he was sick all the way home.

9

IT WAS early evening when the
plane dropped him off in New York Crater, and picked up
another charter. Two cold eggs and some scalding coffee, eaten
standing up at the airport counter. Great for the stomach, but
no time to stop. Anyway, Dan's stomach wasn't in the mood
for dim lights and pale wine, not just this minute. Questions
and recriminations howled through his mind. The knowledge
that he had made the one Class A colossal blunder of his thirty
years in politics, this last half-day. The miscalculation of a
man! He should have known about MacKenzie, or at least
suspected. MacKenzie was getting old, he wanted a Retread,

and wanted it badly. Before, he had figured Dan to get it for him. Then something changed his mind, and he threw in with Rinehart.

Why?

Armstrong's suicide, of course. Pretty good proof that even Rinehart hadn't known it was a suicide. If Carl had brought back evidence of murder, Dan was certain to win, MacKenzie had thought. But evidence of suicide—that was far too shaky. Walt Rinehart had his hooks in too deep to be dislodged by that.

The loudspeaker blared the boarding signal for the Washington Jet. Dan gulped the last of his coffee, and found a visiphone booth with a scrambler in working order. Two calls. The first was to Jean, to line up round-the-clock guards for Peter Golden's widow on Long Island. Jean couldn't keep surprise out of her voice. Dan grunted and didn't elaborate; just get them out there.

Then a call to Carl. He chewed his cigar nervously. Two minutes of waiting while they corralled Carl from wherever he was. Then: "Carl, I just saw MacKenzie. I found him hiding in Rinehart's hip pocket."

"Oh, oh." Carl's face on the screen looked desolate. "Dan, we've got to have time."

"We've got it, but the price was very steep, son."

Silence then as Carl peered at him. "Do you mean what I think you mean?"

"I'm afraid that's what I mean."

"I see."

"Lad, I'll try to make it up to you, somehow, I swear I will," Dan said miserably. "I hated myself, but I was trapped. If I just hadn't been in such a hurry, if I'd only thought it out, but I was trapped. It was an awful error, and every bit of it was my fault."

"Well, don't go out and shoot yourself over it," Carl said.

"I suppose it was bound to happen sooner or later. What about Mother?"

"She'll be perfectly safe. They won't get within a mile of her. Look, son, is Fisher doing all right?"

Carl nodded. "I talked to him an hour ago. He'll be ready for you by tomorrow night, he thinks."

"Sober?"

"Sober. And mad. He was the right guy for the job." Worried lines deepened on Golden's forehead. "Look, Dan, don't worry about—the price. What about you? How did Rinehart take it?"

"It scared him. He'd almost forgotten, I think. You carry on, now. Everything's going to be fine." Dan rang off, scowling. He wished he was as sure as he sounded. It was Rinehart with his back to the wall, now, and Dan wasn't too sure he liked that.

An hour later he landed in Washington, and Jean was dragging him into the Volta. "Dad, if you don't get some sleep now, I'll personally put you out with ether. You're killing yourself. Now shut up while I drive you home."

A soft bed, darkness, escape. When had he slept last? He couldn't remember, but it was like heaven, with no dreams to bother him.

10

HE SLEPT the clock around, over twenty-three hours, which he had not intended, and then caught the next night jet to Las Vegas, which he had intended. There was some delay with the passenger list after he had gone aboard. Somebody raising a howl with the disbursing officer, and the jet took off four minutes late. Dan slept again, fitfully.

Somebody slid down into the adjoining seat like a stealthy shadow. "Well! Good old Dan Fowler!"

A gaunt, frantic-looking man, with skin like cracked parchment across his high cheekbones, and a pair of Dracula eyes looking down at Dan. If Death walked in human flesh, Dan thought, it would look like John Tyndall.

"What do you want, 'Moses'?"

"Just dropped by to chat," said Tyndall. "You're heading for Las Vegas, eh? Why?"

"I like the climate out there," Dan said. "Look, if you want to talk, talk and get it over with."

Tyndall lifted a narrow foot and gave the recline-button a sharp jab, dumping the senator back against the seat. "You've got something cooking, and I like the smell. I want my share, right now."

Dan stared into the gaunt face, and burst out laughing. He had never actually been so close to John Tyndall before, and he did *not* like the smell, which had brought on the laugh, but he knew all about Tyndall. More than Tyndall himself knew, probably. He could even remember the early rallies Tyndall had led, feeding on the fears and suspicions and nasty rumors about rejuvenation that had grown up in the early days. It was evil, they had said. This was not God's way, this was Man's way, as evil as Man was evil. If God had wanted Man to live a thousand years, he would have given him such a body—

Or:

They'll use it for a tool! A political football. They'll buy and sell with it. They'll make a cult of it, they're doing it right now! Look at Walter Rinehart. Did you hear about his scheme? To keep it down to five hundred a year? They'll make themselves a ruling class, an immortal elite, with Rinehart for their Black Pope. Better that *nobody* should have it—

Or:

Immortality, huh? But what kind? You hear what hap-

pened to Harvey Tatum? That's right, the jet-car man, big
business. He was one of that Noble Ten they're always bragging
about. But they say he had to have special drugs every night,
that he had *changed*. That's right, if he didn't get these drugs,
see, he'd go mad and try to suck blood and butcher children.
Oh, they didn't dare publish it, had to put him out of the way
quietly, but my brother-in-law was down in Lancaster one
night when—

All it really needed was the right man, and one day there
was "Moses" Tyndall. Leader of the New Crusade for God.
Small, at first. But the ad-men began supporting him, broadcasting his rallies, playing him up big. Abolish rejuvenation,
it's a blot against Man's immortal soul. Amen. Then the insurance people came along, with money. (The ad-men and the
insurance people weren't too concerned about Man's immortal
soul—they'd take their share now, thanks—but this didn't
bother Tyndall too much. They were misguided, but they were
on God's side. He prayed for them.) So they gave Tyndall the
first Abolitionist seat in the Senate, in 2124, just nine years
ago, and the fight between Rinehart and Dan Fowler that was
brewing even then had turned into a three-cornered fight.

Dan grinned up at Tyndall and said, "Go away, John. Don't
bother me."

"You're on to something," Tyndall snarled. "What is your
flunky Carl Golden nosing around the Tenner Agency for?
Why the heat on Metro Insurance? Why the sudden bounding
interest in Nevada? Two trips in three days, what are you
trying to track down?"

"Why should I tell *you* anything, Holy Man?"

The parchment face wrinkled unpleasantly. "Because it
would be very smart of you if you did, that's why. Rinehart's
out of it now. Washed up, finished, thanks to you. Now it's
just you or me, one or the other. You're in my way, and
you're going to be gotten out of my way when you've finished

up Rinehart, because that's when I'm really going to start rolling. Go along with me now and you won't get smashed, Dan."

"Get out of here," Dan snarled, sitting bolt upright. "You gave the same story to Carl, a long time ago when he was with you, remember? Carl's my boy now—do you think I'll swallow the same bait?"

"You'd be smart if you did." The man leaned forward. "I'll let you in on a secret. I've had a—vision—you might say. There are going to be riots and fires and shouting, around the time of the Hearings. People will be killed. Lots of people —spontaneous outbursts of passion, of course, the great voice of the people rising against the Abomination. And against *you*, Dan. A few Repeaters may be taken out and hanged, and then when you have won against Rinehart, you'll find people thinking that you're really a traitor."

"Nobody will swallow that," Dan snapped.

"Just watch and see. I can still call it off, if you say so." He stood up quickly as Dan's face went purple. "New Chicago," he said smoothly. "Have to see a man here, and then get back to the Capitol. Happy hunting, Dan. You know where to reach me."

He strode down the aisle of the ship, leaving Dan staring bleakly at an empty seat.

Paul, Paul—

11

HE MET Terry Fisher at the landing field in Las Vegas. A firm handshake, clear brown eyes looking at him the way a four-year-old looks at Santa Claus. "Glad you could come tonight, Senator. I've had a busy

couple of days. I think you'll be interested." Remarkable restraint in the man's voice. His face was full of things unsaid.
Dan caught it; he knew faces, read them like typescript.

"What is it, son?"

"Wait until you see." Fisher laughed nervously. "I almost
thought for a while that I was back on Mars."

"Cigar?"

"No thanks. I never use them."

The car broke through darkness across bumpy desert pave-
ment. The men sat silently. Then a barbed wire enclosure
loomed up, and a guard walked over, peered at their creden-
tials, and waved them through. Ahead lay a long, low row of
buildings, and a tall something spearing up into the clear
desert night, two hundred yards away—the Starship itself.
They stopped at the first building, and hurried up the steps.

Small, red-faced Lijinsky greeted them, all warm handshake
and enthusiasm and unmistakable happiness and surprise. "A
real pleasure, Senator! We haven't had a direct governmental
inspection for quite a while. I'm glad I'm here to show you
around."

"Everything is going right along, eh?"

"Oh, yes! She'll be a ship to be proud of. Now, I think we
can arrange quarters for you, and in the morning we can sit
down and have a nice, long talk."

Terry Fisher was shaking his head. "I think the senator
wants to see the ship *now*—isn't that right, Senator?"

Lijinsky's eyes opened wide, his head bobbing in surprise.
Young-old creases on his face flickered. "Tonight? Well, of
course, if you insist, but it's almost two in the morning! We
only have a skeleton crew working at night. Tomorrow you
could see—"

"Tonight, if you don't mind." Dan tried to keep the sharp
edge out of his voice. "Unless you have some specific objection."

"Objection? No—" Lijinsky seemed puzzled, and a little hurt. But he bounced back: "Tonight it is, then. Let's go." There was no doubting the little man's honesty. He wasn't hiding anything, just surprised. But a moment later there was concern on his face as he lead them out toward the towering scaffolds. "There's no question about appropriations, I hope, Senator?"

"No, no. Nothing of the sort."

"Well, I'm certainly glad to hear that. But I can't help worrying. Sometimes our contacts from Washington are a little disappointed in the ship, you know."

Dan's throat tightened. "Why?"

"No reason, really. We're making fine progress, it isn't that. Yes, things really buzz around here; just ask Mr. Fisher about *that*. He was here all day watching the workers. But there are always minor changes in plans, of course, as we recognize more of the problems."

Terry Fisher grimaced silently, and followed them into a small Whirlwind groundcar. The little gyro-car bumped down the road on its single wheel, down into a gorge, then out onto the flats. Dan strained his eyes, peering ahead at the spear of Starship gleaming in the distant night lights. Paragraphs from the last Starship Progress Report flickered through his mind, and a frown gathered as they came closer to the ship. Then the car halted on the edge of the building-pit and they blinked up and down at the scaffolded monster.

Dan didn't even get out of the car. He just stared. The Progress Report had featured photos, protected testing dates, even ventured a possible date for launching, with the building of the Starship so near to completion. That had been a month ago. Now Dan stared at the ship and shook his head, uncomprehending.

The hull plates were off again, lying in heaps on the ground in a mammoth circle. The ship was a skeleton, a long, gawky structure of naked metal beams. Even now in the bright flood-lights a dozen men were scampering around the scaffolding, before Dan's incredulous eyes, and he saw a huge beam coming *off* the body of the ship, being grappled by the crane and slowly, slowly lowered to the ground.

Ten years ago the ship had looked the same. As he watched, he felt a wave of hopelessness sweep through him, a sense of desolate, empty bitterness. Ten years—

His eyes met Terry Fisher's in the gloom of the car, begging to be told it wasn't so. Fisher shook his head.

Then Dan said: "I think I've seen enough. Take me back to the air field. You'd better come, too, Terry."

Later, as the return jet speared east into the dawn, Terry Fisher said, "It was the same thing on Mars. The constant re-fining and super-refining of plans, the slowing down of every-thing, the subtle change in viewpoint. I went up there ready to beat the world barehanded, to work on the frontier, to build that colony and maybe even lead off to start another one. I ac-tually worked out plans of my own for a breakaway colony. I figured we were going to need colony builders when we went on out to the stars." He shrugged sadly. "Carl told you, I guess. They looked at my plans very carefully, and discussed them in council, and worked out alternatives, and polled the whole colony, and accepted volunteers for a planning committee, and then Barness decided that it was really too early to *do* anything about it. Maybe in another ten years. Too much work already, with just one colony. And there *was* too much work, in a sense: frantic activity, noise, hubbub, confusion, fancy plans—all going nowhere. No drive, no real direction." He shrugged again. "Pretty soon I saw that nothing was going to happen, my plan was just quietly going to die, like everything else on Mars."

"Nobody saw it happening?"

"It wasn't the sort of thing you could see. You could only *feel* it. It started when Armstrong came back to the colony, rejuvenated, to take over its development. Personally, I think Armstrong *did* finally see it. I think that's why he suicided."

"But the Starship," Dan cried. "It was almost built, and there they were, *tearing it down.*"

"Ah, yes. For the twenty-seventh time, I believe. A change in the engineering thinking, that's all. Keller and Lijinsky suddenly came to the conclusion that the whole thing might fall apart in midair at the launching. Can you imagine it? We've been building rockets for years, running them to Mars every two months! But they could pinpoint the flaw on paper, and prove it on the computers, and by the time they got through explaining it every soul in the whole administrative staff was going around saying yes, by golly, they're right, it *might* fall apart at the launching unless we make these changes. Why, it's a standing joke among the workers there. They call Lijinsky Old Jet Propulsion and it's always good for a laugh. But then, Keller and Stark and Lijinsky ought to know what they're doing. They've all been rejuvenated, and have been working on the ship for years." Fisher's voice was heavy with anger.

Dan didn't answer. There wasn't anything to say, and he just couldn't tell Terry Fisher how it felt to have a cold blanket of fear wrapping around his heart, so dreadful and cold that he hardly dared look five minutes into the future right now, with Paul's words echoing in his ears: *we have a monster on our hands.*

12

HE WAS sick when they reached Washington. The pain in his chest became acute as he started walking down the gangway, and by the time he found a seat in the terminal and popped a nitro-tablet under his tongue he was breathing in deep, ragged gasps. He sat very still, trying to lean back against the seat, and suddenly he realized that he was very, very ill. The good red-headed Dr. Moss would smile in satisfaction, he thought bitterly. Sweat came out on his forehead; it had never seemed very likely to him that he might one day die. He didn't *have* to die in this great, wonderful world of new bodies for old, he could live on, and on, and on. He could live to see the Golden Centuries of Man. A solar system teeming with life. Ships to challenge the stars, the barriers breaking, crumbling before their very eyes. Other changes, as short-lived Man became long-lived Man. Changes in teaching, in thinking, in feeling. Disease, the Enemy, was crushed. Famine, the Enemy, was slinking back into the dim memory of history. War, the Enemy, now made pointless to extinction.

All based on one principle: that Man should live if he could. He need not die. If a man could live forty years instead of twenty, had it been wrong to battle the plagues that struck him down in his youth? If he could live sixty years instead of forty, had the great researchers of the 1940s and '50s and '60s been wrong? Was it any more wrong now to want to live a thousand years? Who could say that it was?

Dan took a shuddering breath, nodded to Terry Fisher, and walked unsteadily to the cab stand. He would not believe what he had seen at Starship Project. It was not enough to draw any conclusions. Collect *all* the evidence, *then* conclude. When Fisher took his elbow, he gave him an ashen smile. "It's nothing. The ticker kicks up once in a while, that's all. Let's go see what Carl and Jean and the boys have dug up."

Carl and Jean and the boys had dug up plenty. The floor of Dan's headquarters was covered with paper, carbons, punch cards and rubble. A dozen people were working here and there with tapes, typewriters, telephones, papers, program cards. Jean met them at the door, hustled them into the private offices in the back. "Carl just got here, too. He's down eating. The boys outside are trying to make sense out of his insurance and advertising figures."

"He got next to them okay?"

"Sure, but you were right, they didn't like it."

"What sort of reports?"

The girl sighed. "Most of the stuff is still being analyzed, which makes it hard to evaluate. The ad-men have to be figuring what they're going to be doing in the next half-century, so that they'll be there with the right thing when the time comes. But they don't like what they see. People have to buy what the ad-men are selling, or the ad-men are out of business, and already they see a dangerous trend. People aren't in such a rush to buy as they once were. They don't have the same sense of urgency that they used to—" Her hands fluttered. "Well, as I say, it's all up in the air. Analysis will be in by morning. The matter of suicides is a little more tangible: the rates are up, all over. But break it down into first-generation and Re-peaters, and it's pretty clear what's happening."

"Like Armstrong," said Dan slowly.

Jean nodded. "Oh, here's Carl now."

Carl came in, rubbing his hands, and gave Dan a queer look. "Everything under control, Dan?"

Dan nodded. He told Carl about Tyndall's proposition. Carl gave a wry grin. "He hasn't changed a bit, has he?"

"Yes, he has. He's gotten lots stronger."

Carl scowled, and slapped the desk with his palm. "You should have stopped him, Dan. I told you that a long time ago, back when I first met you. He was aiming for your throat even then, trying to use me and what I knew about Dad to sell the country a pack of lies about you. He almost did, too. I hated your guts back then. I thought you were the rottenest man who had ever come up in politics, until you got hold of me and pounded some sense into my head. And Tyndall's never forgiven you *that*, either."

"All right. We're still ahead of him. Have you finished with the ad-men?"

"Oh, no. I just got back from a trip south. My nose is still cold."

Dan's eyebrows went up. "Antarctica? And how was Dr. Aviado? I haven't seen any reports from his solar energy project for five years."

"Yes you have, you just couldn't read them. Aviado is quite a theoretician. That's how he got his money and his Project, down there, with plenty of room to build his reflectors and his plates and his batteries, with nobody around to get hurt except a few penguins if something went wrong. And he's done a real job of development down there since his rejuvenation."

"Ah." Dan glanced up hopefully.

"Now there," said Carl, "is a real lively project. Solar energy into power on a utilitarian level. The man is a fanatic, of course, but with his plans and his plant he *could* actually be producing in another five years." He looked bleakly at the senator.

"Could?"

"He could—except that he's gotten sidetracked a bit," said Carl.

Dan glanced at Terry Fisher. "How?"

"Well, his equipment is working fine, and he can concentrate solar heat from ten square miles onto a spot the size of a manhole cover. But he hasn't started converting it to useful power yet." Carl suddenly burst out laughing. "Dan, this will kill you. Billions and billions of calories of solar heat concentrated down there, and do you know what he's doing with it? He's melting a hole in the ice two thousand feet deep and a mile wide, that's what."

"A hole in the ice!"

"Exactly. Conversion? Certainly, but first he wants to be sure his technique is perfect. So right now he and his whole crew are very busy *trying to melt down Antarctica*. And if you give him another ten years, he's just liable to do it, too!"

13

THIS WAS the last, most painful trip of all.

Dan didn't even know why he was going, except that Paul had told him he should go, and he could not risk leaving a single stone unturned.

The landing in New York Crater had been rough, and Dan had cracked his elbow on the bulkhead; he nursed it now as he left the Volta on the deserted street of the crater city, and entered the low one-story lobby of the groundscraper. The clerk took his name impassively, and he sat down to wait.

An hour passed, then another.

Then: "Mr. Devlin will see you now, Senator."

Down in the elevator, fifteen—sixteen—seventeen stories. Above him was the world; here, deep below, with subtly efficient ventilators and shafts and exotic cubbyholes for retreat, a man could forget that a world even existed up above.

Soft lighting in the corridor, a golden plastic door. The door swung open, and a tiny old man blinked out.

"Mr. Chauncey Devlin?"

"Senator Fowler!" The little old man beamed. "Come in, come in. My dear fellow, if I'd realized it was you, I'd never have kept you so long." He smiled, obviously distressed. "Retreat has its disadvantages, too, you see. Nothing is perfect but life, as they say. When *you've* lived for a hundred and ninety years, you'll be glad to get away from people, and be able to keep them out, from time to time."

In better light Dan stared openly at the man. A hundred and ninety years. It was incredible. He said as much.

"Isn't it, though?" Chauncey Devlin chirped. "Well, I was a war baby! Can you imagine? Born in London in 1945. But I don't even think about those horrid years any more. Imagine —barbarians dropping bombs on each other!"

A tiny bird of a man, three times rejuvenated, and still the mind was sharp, the eyes were sharp. The face was a strange mixture of recent youth and very great age. It stirred something deep inside Dan—almost a feeling of loathing. An uncanny feeling.

"My daughter and I, we've always known your music," Dan said. "We've always loved it. Just a week ago we heard the Washington Philharmonic doing—"

"The eighth." Chauncey Devlin cut him off disdainfully. "They always do the eighth."

"It's a great symphony," Dan protested.

Devlin chuckled, and bounced about the room like a little boy. "It was only half finished when they chose me for the big plunge," he said. "Of course I was doing a lot of conducting then, too. Now I'd much rather just write." He hurried across the long, softly lit room to the piano, came back with a sheaf of manuscript, "Do you read music? This is what I've been doing recently. Can't get it quite right, but it'll come, it'll come."

"Which will this be?" asked Dan.

"The tenth. The ninth was almost done when I was rejuvenated. I finished it during my year as Free Agent. Strictly a potboiler, I'm afraid. I thought it was pretty good at the time, but *this* one—ah!" He fondled the smooth sheets of paper. "In this one I could *say* something. Always before, it was hit and run, make a stab at it, then rush on to stab at something else, never time enough to do *anything* right. But not *this* one." He patted the manuscript happily. "With this one there will be *nothing* wrong."

"It's almost finished?"

"Oh, no. Oh, my goodness no! A fairly acceptable first movement, but even that's not what it *will* be when I'm finished."

"I see. I—understand. And you've been working on it—how long?"

"Oh, I don't know—I must have it down here somewhere. Oh, yes. It was begun in April of 2057. Just seventy-seven years."

They talked on, until it was too painful to continue. Dan thanked his host, and started back for the corridor and life again. He had never even mentioned why he had come, and nobody had noticed.

Chauncey Devlin, a tiny, perfect wax image of a man, so old, so wise, so excited and full of enthusiasm and energy and carefulness, working eagerly, happily—

And accomplishing nothing. *Seventy-seven years*. The picture of a man with a great mind, slowly grinding to a standstill!

And now Dan Fowler knew that he hadn't really been looking at Chauncey Devlin at all. He had been looking at the whole human race.

14
FEBRUARY 15, 2135.

The day of the Hearings, to consider the charges and petition formally placed before the Senate by The Honorable Daniel Fowler, Independent Senator from the great state of Illinois. The long oval hearing room was filling early; the gallery above was packed by 9:05 in the morning. TV boys all over the place. The Criterion Committee members, taking their places in twos and threes, some old, some young, some rejuvenated, some not, sitting down at one end of the oval. Then the other senators—not the President, of course, but he'll be well represented by Senator Rinehart himself, ah yes. Don't worry about the President.

Bad news in the papers. Trouble in New Chicago, where so much trouble seems to start these days. Bomb thrown into the lobby of the Hoffman Medical Center out there, a *bomb* of all things! Shades of Lenin. Couple of people killed, and one of the doctors nearly beaten to death on the street before the police arrived to clear the mob away. Dan Fowler's name popping up here and there, not pleasantly. Whispers and accusations, *sotto voce*. And "Moses" Tyndall's network hookup last night—of course nobody with any sense listens to *him,* but did you hear that hall go wild?

Rinehart—yes, that's him. Well, he's got a right to look worried. If Dan can unseat him here and now, he's washed up. According to the rules of the government, you know, Fowler can legally petition for Rinehart's chairmanship without risking it as a platform plank in the next election, and then if the Senate votes him in after the Hearings, he's got the election made. Dan's smart. They're scared to throw old Rinehart out, of course. After all, he's let them keep their thumbs on rejuvenation all these years with his criteria, and if they supported him they got named, and if they didn't, they didn't get named. Not as simple as that, of course, but that's what it boiled down to, let me tell you! But now, if they reject Dan's petition and the people give him the election over their heads, they're *really* in a spot. Dan wants that chairmanship—

How's that? Can't be too long now. Look there, Tyndall just came in, Bible and all! Let's see if he's got any tomatoes in his pockets. Ol' "Moses" really gets you going—ever listen to him talk? Well, it's just as well. Damn, but it's hot in here—

In the rear chamber, Dan mopped his brow, popped a pill under his tongue, puffed savagely on the long black cigar. "You with me, lad?"

Carl nodded.

"You know what it means."

"I don't care what it means. I'm with you. There's your buzzer, better get in there." Carl turned back to Jean and the others around the 80-inch screen, set deep in the wall. Dan put his cigar down, gently, as though he planned to be back to smoke it again before it went out, and then walked through the tall oak doors.

The murmur in the gallery above rose to a roar of applause as he was recognized, and suddenly someone was on his feet, and then another, and the whole gallery rose in a standing ovation. Dan waved and took his seat, grinned across at Senator Libby, leaned his head over to drop an aside into Parker's ear. Rinehart sat with a face of stone as the applause died and a gavel banged and the president of the Senate said, "Will the clerk please read the charges and petition that concern this chamber this morning," and then the charges, read off in a droning nasal voice—

—Whereas the criteria for selection of candidates for subtotal prosthesis, first written by the Honorable Walter Rinehart, senator from the great state of Alaska, have been found to be inadequate, outdated, and utterly inappropriate to the use of this life-sustaining technique that is now possible—

—And whereas that same Honorable Walter Rinehart has repeatedly used these criteria, not in the just, honorable, and humble way in which such criteria must be regarded, but rather as a tool and weapon for his own furtherance and for that of his friends and associates—

Dan waited, patiently, as the voice droned on. Was Rinehart's face whiter than before? Was the hall quieter now? Maybe not, but wait for the petition—

—The Senate of the United States of North America is formally petitioned that the Honorable Walter Rinehart should be dismissed from his seat as chairman of the Criterion Committee, and that his seat should be yielded to the Honorable Daniel Fowler, senator from the great state of Illinois and author of this petition, who has pledged himself before God to seek, through this committee in any and every way possible, the extension of the benefits of subtotal prosthesis to all the people of this land and not to a chosen few—

Screams, hoots, catcalls, wild applause, all from the gallery. None below—senatorial dignity forbade. And then Dan Fowler stood up (an older Dan Fowler than most of them seemed to remember) and requested the floor. And they listened, incredulous, as the familiar, rasping voice rose in the hall: "You have all heard the charges which have been read. I now stand before you, formally, *in order to withdraw them.*"

Slowly then, measuring every word, he told them. He knew that words were not enough, but he told them. "Only 70,000 men and women have undergone the process, at this date, out of over five hundred million people on this continent, yet already it has begun to sap our strength. We were told that no changes were involved, and indeed we saw no changes, but changes were there. The suicides of men like Kenneth Armstrong did not just happen. There are many reasons that might lead a man to take his life in this world of ours—selfishness, self-pity, hatred of the world or of himself, guilt, bitterness, resentment—but it was none of these that motivated Kenneth Armstrong. *His death was the act of a bewildered, defeated mind*, for he saw what I am telling you now and knew that it was true. He saw Starships built and rebuilt, and never launched. He saw colonies dying of lethargy, because there was no longer any drive behind them. He saw brilliant minds losing sight of goals and drifting into endless inconsequential digressions, lifetimes wasted in repetition, in re-doing and re-writing and re-living. He saw what I too can see: a vicious downward spiral which can only lead to death for all of us in the last days.

"This is why I withdraw the charges and petition of this Hearing. This is why I reject rejuvenation, and declare that it is a monstrous thing *which we must not allow to continue*. This is why I now announce that I personally will nominate the Honorable John Tyndall, senator from the great state of Los Angeles, for President in the elections next spring, and will pledge him my support, my political organization, my experience, and my every personal effort to see that he wins that election."

15

IT SEEMED there would be no
end to it, when Dan Fowler had finished. "Moses" Tyndall
sat staring as the blood drained out of his sallow face; his jaw
gaped, and he half-rose from his chair, then sank back with
a ragged cough, staring at the senator as if Dan had been
transformed into a snake. Carl and Terry were beside Dan in
a moment, clearing a way back to the rear chambers, then
down the steps of the building to a cab. Senator Libby inter-
cepted them there, his face purple with rage, Dwight Mac-
Kenzie, bristling and indignant, in his wake. "You've lost your
mind, Dan, you've simply—"

"I have not. I am perfectly sane."

"But Tyndall! He'll turn Washington into a grand revival
meeting, he'll—"

"Then we'll cut him down to size. He's *my* candidate, remember. He'll play my game if it pays him well enough. But I want
an Abolitionist administration, and I'm going to have one."

Libby was shaking his head. "There isn't a sane man in the
country who'll support you. You'll be whipped so badly you'll
never win another election."

Dan ground out his cigar under his heel, and started down
the steps. "Fine. Then I'll fight it after I'm beaten. And when
it comes to a fight, I'm no slouch."

In the cab he stared glumly out the window, his heart racing,
his whole body shaking in reaction now. "You know what it
means," he said to Carl for the tenth time.

"Yes, Dan, I know."

"It means no rejuvenation, for you or for any of us. It
means proving something to people that they just don't want

to believe, it means cramming it down their throats if we have to. It means taking away their right to keep on living."

"I know all that."

"Carl, if you want out, you, or anybody, now's the time."

"Correction. Yesterday was the time."

"Okay then. We've got work to do."

16

UP IN the offices again, Dan was on the phone immediately. He knew politics, and people, like the jungle cat knows the whimpering creatures he stalks. He knew that it was the first impact, the first jolting blow that would win for them, or lose for them. Everything had to hit right. He had spent his life working with people, building friends, building power, banking his resources, investing himself. Now the time had come to cash in his investment.

Carl and Jean and the others worked with him—a dreadful afternoon and evening, fighting off newsmen, blocking phone calls, trying to concentrate in the midst of bedlam. They labored to set up a work schedule, listing names, outlining telegrams, drinking coffee, as Dan swore at his dead cigar like old times once again, and grinned like a madman as the plans slowly developed and blossomed. The snowball was rolling.

Then the phone jangled, and Dan reached out for it, and it was that last small effort that did it. A sledge-hammer blow, from deep within him, sharp agonizing pain, a driving hunger for the air that he just couldn't pull into his lungs. He let out a small, sharp cry, and doubled over with pain. They found him seconds later, still clinging to the phone, his breath so faint as to be no breath at all.

He regained consciousness hours later. He stared about him at the straight lines of the ceiling, at the hospital bed and the hospital window. Dimly he saw Carl Golden, head drooping on his chest, dozing at the side of the bed.

There was a hissing sound, and he raised a hand, felt the oxygen mask over his mouth and nose. Even with that help, every breath was an agony of pain and weariness.

He was so very tired. But slowly, through the fog, he remembered. Cold sweat broke out on his forehead, drenched his body. *He was alive.* Yet he remembered clearly the thought that had exploded in his mind in the instant the blow had come. *I'm dying. This is the end—it's too late now.* And then, cruelly, *why did I wait so long?*

He struggled against the mask, sat bolt upright in bed. "I'm going to die," he whispered, then caught his breath. Carl sat up, smiled at him.

"Lie back, Dan. Get some rest."

Had he heard? Had Carl heard the fear he had whispered? Perhaps not. He lay back, panting, as Carl watched. Do you know what I'm thinking, Carl? I'm thinking how much I want to live. People don't *need* to die—wasn't that what Dr. Moss had said? It's such a terrible waste, he had said.

Too late, now. Dan's hands trembled. He remembered the senators in the oval hall, the people in the gallery, the brave words he had shouted. He remembered Rinehart's face, and Tyndall's, and Libby's. He was committed now. Yesterday, no. Now, yes.

Paul had been right, and Dan had proved it.

His eyes moved across to the bedside table. A telephone. He was still alive, Moss had said that sometimes it was possible *even when you were dying.* That was what they did with your father, wasn't it, Carl? Brave Peter Golden, who had fought Rinehart so hard, who had begged and pleaded for universal rejuvenation, waited and watched to catch Rinehart red-handed, to prove that he was corrupting the law and expose him. Simple, honest Peter Golden, applying so naively for his rightful place on the list, when his cancer was diagnosed. And then the auto accident, never *definitely* linked to Rinehart, but no real *accident* either. Peter Golden had been all but dead when he had finally whispered his defeat, begging for help and giving Rinehart his pledge of perpetual silence in return for life. They had snatched him from death, indeed. But he had been crucified all the same. The life they had given him had been a living death, which was why in just a few short months he had quietly withdrawn and curled up and died once and for all, in spite of his rejuvenation, loathing himself for his betrayal of all he believed in. And you watched it all, didn't you, Carl? You and your mother watched him die, inch by inch, and couldn't find a way to help him. Rinehart had stripped him of everything and found a coward and traitor underneath.

Coward? Why? Was it wrong to want to live? Dan Fowler was dying. Why must it be he? He had committed himself to a fight, yes, but there were others, young men, who could fight. Men like Peter Golden's son.

But you're their leader, Dan. If you fail them, they will never win.

Carl was watching him silently, his lean dark face expressionless. Could the boy read his mind? Was it possible that he knew what Dan Fowler was thinking? Carl had understood before. It had seemed sometimes that Carl understood Dan far better than Dan did. He wanted to cry out to Carl now, spill over his dreadful thoughts, but he knew he could not do it.

There was no one to run to. He was facing himself now. No more cover-up, no deceit. Life or death, that was the choice. No compromise. Life or death, but decide *now*. Not tomororw, not next week, not in five minutes—

Now.

And there was the flaw, the one thing that even Paul hadn't known, perhaps the universal flaw: that given the choice, a man will choose life. That life is too dear, that a man loves life—not what he can do with life, but life itself for its own sake—too much to choose to die. There was no choice, not really. A man will *always* choose life, as long as the choice is really his. Dan Fowler knew that now.

It would be selling himself, as Peter Golden did. It would betray Carl, and Jean, and all the rest. It would mean derision, and scorn, and oblivion for Dan Fowler.

Sorry. But that was the way it had to be—

Had to be?

The pain began again in his chest.

He looked at the telephone on the bedside stand. An easy arm's length away. Reach out, pick up the receiver, a single call to Dr. Moss. So easy—

As easy as crossing back across the gulf from Death. That flaw—universal? Maybe not. There were others, throughout history, who had chosen the other path when the cause was great enough. Martyrs, all of them. But what comfort to be a living traitor?

He looked again at the telephone as the pain swelled up, almost overwhelmed him. His hand moved toward it, almost involuntarily. "Carl. *Carl!* Help me! Hold my hand back!"

"Gently, Dan." Carl held his hand.

"You know what I mean."

"Yes, I know. But I don't need to hold your hand, do I? Not *yours*—"

The pain swept higher and this time did not stop. "No, lad, not mine," Dan breathed, as Carl felt the tension in his arm relax, and his hand go limp. And in the last flickering instant before the darkness, *"Thank you, lad."*

17

JEAN FOWLER came into the room moments later as Carl Golden wept, silently and tearlessly. She stared at Dan, grey on the bed, and then at Carl. One look at Carl's face and she knew too.

Carl nodded, slowly. "I'm sorry, Jean."

She shook her head, tears welling up. "But you loved him so."

"More than my own father."

"Then why didn't you *make* him call?"

"He wanted to be immortal. Always, that drove him. Greatness, power, all the same. Now he will be immortal, because he knew we needed a martyr in order to win. Now we will win. The other way, he knew we would surely lose, and he would live on and on and on and die every day." He turned slowly to the bed and brought the sheet up gently. "Maybe this is better, who can say? This way he will never die."

Together they left the quiet room.

PART TWO

Psi High

1

THE ALIEN'S ship skimmed down like a shadow from the outer atmosphere and settled gently and silently in the tangled underbrush of a hillside overlooking a bend in the broad river. There was the hiss of scorched leaves, the piping of a small, trapped animal—then silence. It was dusk, with the sunlight just departing the hilltops around; here in the cut leading down to the river the gloom of darkness was settling.

Somewhere across the hills a dog howled mournfully. Night birds made small rustling sounds through the scrub and underbrush. The alien waited, alert and tense, but he was not listening for audible sounds. If his race had ever possessed hearing, it was long since lost; they had no need to hear. Instead he sat with his cold yellow eyes half closed, waiting to feel any flickering touch deep in his mind, any whisper of surprise or wonder or fear that his powerful thought-receptors might pick up from the dark hills around the ship. Because that, above all, was

77

critical: that his arrival here be entirely undetected. *Everything* depended on that.

He waited and waited as no thought-fingers came to touch him. At last he relaxed, grunted his satisfaction and scorn. Foolish of him to worry. On *his* world, any unidentified ship approaching within two light years of their sun would be detected and destroyed without hesitation or mercy. No such technology here, and even if the stupid cattle-people who lived here had seen his ship, they wouldn't believe it. The alien stretched back against the couch, allowing his long, tight muscles to relax. Scouts had landed here a dozen times before, and always the reports were the same: the natives thought ships such as his were a delusion, figments of their own imaginations! No, there would be no problem here when his work was finished and the full-scale invasion began. Already the preliminary studies were completed, the plans worked out in the finest detail; and then, soon, his people would be rich with food and slaves once again, and he would be the honored one! Perhaps he would even be allowed to touch the robe of the leader himself! He gloated in anticipation. There was no possible flaw, no way these dull, cowering Man-things could detect or hinder the secret, silent invasion that would come, except for one thing—

The thing he was here, alone, to evaluate.

A people without psi-presence were helpless to defend themselves against a race of powerful telepaths such as his. They would not even know they were being invaded until they were overwhelmed. This planet was a primitive world, indeed, with a ludicrously primitive people, but some few of them had psi-presence already developing. Crude, rudimentary, feeble, but just possibly enough to throw invasion plans awry.

That was what the alien had to find out: how much, how strong, the power to enter other minds might be, in these people. *For psi-presence could detect other psi-presence, always, anywhere, despite any disguise.* The alien knew that. It was the one universal denominator in all the ages of conquest, plundering and enslavement that had made his people the cruel masters of half a galaxy. Before they dared to come in force, they must know the strength of the psi-presence on this world, the one weapon that could possibly defeat them.

The alien moved, finally, beginning his preparations. In the center of the cabin an image flickered, swarming flecks of light and shadow that filled out a three-dimensional form, a complete and detailed model of one of the Man-things that populated this planet. The alien sat back and studied the image carefully through hooded yellow eyes. There must be no mistake, not here, not now. The scouts had been here and returned, bringing back the necessary data and a dozen or more specimens of the Man-things that lived long enough for the laboratories to dissect their minds and bodies and work out satisfactory models for disguise. Now as he stared at the image, studying the bone structure and muscle contour, the alien marveled at the skill of the lab staff—an almost perfect replica! Slowly, following the model, he began to work with the plasti-flesh, molding the sharp angles of his members into puffy Man-like curves, skillfully laying the folds of skin, forming muscle bulges and jointed fingers, always studying the image of the strange, clumsy creature flickering in the cabin before him.

The image of a Man. That was what they called themselves. There were many of them, and somewhere among them there was psi-presence, feeble and underdeveloped, but *there*, somewhere. He eyed the image again, and pressed a stud on the control panel. Another image met his eyes, an electronic reflection of himself. He studied it, then carefully superimposed the two, adding contours here and there, quick eyes seeking out imperfections as he worked. There must be no mistake. He knew what failure would mean for him—the ultimate disgrace and then slow, painful death by dissociation and destruction of his psi-power neuron by neuron. The leader did not tolerate failures.

At last, satisfied, he stared again at the image, and then at himself. Not quite right—the skin tone was wrong, the yellow came through too clearly in places, and the scouts had reported that that color seemed to carry unpleasant connotations in this culture, for some reason. Any shade of sickly pink, shading into brown and on to black was fine. He worked more brownish-pink pigment into his soft, wrinkle-free skin, then further molded out the cheeks and forehead. Hair would be a problem of course, but then there would be many small imperfections. He smiled grimly to himself. No problem there—in dealing with these stupid minds, there would be other ways to mask imperfections.

Finally the task was done. He had no way to bring a reddish color into his pale green lips, nor to create the myriad wrinkles and creases that criss-crossed the skin of the Man-things, but with his psi-power it did not matter, he would simply project those things into their minds. Rising, the alien struggled into the tight, restricting clothes that lay in a bundle, carefully folded and pressed, at his feet. The boardlike shoes cut into his flesh— he had nothing to correspond to a moveable human ankle—and the hairy fabric of the red-and-white checked skirt made him writhe in discomfort, but once outside the ship he was glad for the warmth. He stepped out onto the ground, and listened again, carefully. Then he made certain arrangements with wires, and threw a switch on a small black panel near the entry port, and began walking stiffly down the hill away from the ship.

He would no longer need the ship. Not now.

It was quite dark. The underbrush grew thicker, and he fought his way through the scrub until he reached a roadway. It was not even paved—incredible! To think some of the scouts had feared such simple, primitive barbarians might actually attempt to oppose them! Yet the reports insisted that far to the east there were great stone and steel cities, the places-of-madness, the scouts had called them. Well, perhaps. *He* certainly saw no stone or steel, only dust and the ruts of wagon wheels. He was aware only of darkness, and a light wind coming up, and the howling of some night beast somewhere over the hill.

The alien trudged on for almost an hour, trying to acclimate his legs to the fierce tug of gravity that pulled at him. And then he stopped short, and listened. . . .

He heard them, then, in the depths of his mind, somewhere very near on the other side of the hill—two Man-things, beyond doubt. No psi-presence there, but at least a contact, perhaps weak and isolated enough to be killed for food. Other mental whispers, too—dull, stupid, vagrant half-thoughts flickering through his mind. Lower life forms, no doubt. Possibly this was a farm, with work animals. The scouts had said there were such. He turned off the road, and almost cried out when the sharp barbs of a fence cut through his tender skin. A trickle of green dripped down his arm, until he rubbed a poultice across it, and it became smooth and sickly pink again. In a burst of rage he pulled the fence out, post and all, and left it on the ground, moving through the woods in the direction of the Man-things he had heard.

Soon the woods ended and he saw the dwelling across a broad clearing. Black dirt lay open in the moonlight. He started across. There was light inside the dwelling, and the dull, babbling flow of uncontrolled Man-thought struck his mind like a vapor. There were other buildings, too—dark buildings, and one tall one with a spoked wheel on top that creaked and rustled in the darkness.

He had almost reached the dwelling when a small, four-legged creature leaped out of the darkness at him, crying out in a horrible discordant barrage. The creature came running swiftly, and the alien's mind caught the sharp whine of fear and hate emanating from the thing. It stopped before him, baring its fangs and snarling. The alien lashed his foot out savagely; it crunched into flesh and bone, and the creature lay flopping helplessly, spurting dark wet stuff, its cry cut off in mid-yelp. The alien stepped onto the porch as the door opened, suddenly, framing a tall, thin Man-thing in a box of yellow light. "Brownie?" a voice called. "Come here, Brownie! What's the matter—" His words trailed off as he saw the alien. "Who are you?"

"A traveler," said the alien, his voice grating harshly in the darkness. "I need lodging and food."

The farmer's eyes narrowed suspiciously as he peered from the doorway. "Where are you from? Come into the light, here, let me get a look at you."

The alien stepped closer, concentrating all his psi-power on the farmer's mind, blurring his perception of the minute imperfections of his disguise. It was far harder than he had expected, it required all his concentration, and he had none left to probe the farmer's mind. No problem, though, he thought as he waited, trembling. That would come later.

The farmer blinked, and nodded, finally. "Well, all right then," he grumbled. "I suppose we can find some food for you. Come on in." And he stepped back for the alien to enter.

2 SECRETARY OF Medical Affairs Benjamin Towne slammed his cane down on the floor with a snarl, and eased himself back in his seat, staring angrily around the small Federal Security Commission anteroom. His

aide, a Cabinet attache standing near the door, retrieved the cane and handed it back to Towne with a polite murmur, then regretted his action instantly when the secretary began whacking it against his palm, short staccato slaps that rang out ominously in the small room. The secretary was not in the habit of waiting; he did not like it in the least, and made no effort to conceal his feelings. His little green cat eyes roved around the room in sharp disapproval, resting momentarily on the neat autodesk, on the cool grey walls, on the vaguely disturbing watercolor on the wall—one of those nauseating Psi-High experimentals that the snob critics seemed to think were so wonderful. The secretary growled and blinked at the morning sunlight streaming through the muted glass panels of the northeast wall. Far below, the second morning rush hour traffic buzzed through the city with frantic nervousness.

The secretary tapped his cane on the floor, glancing up at his aide. "That Sanders girl," he snapped. "Give me her file again."

The aide opened a large briefcase, produced a thick bundle of papers in a manila folder. Towne took them, and glanced through the papers, chewing his lower lip. "How about Dr. Abrams and the rest of the Hoffman Center crowd that are involved? Were they questioned?"

The aide nodded in embarrassment. "We tried, but they ran us around in circles."

Towne's scowl deepened. "Did you give him the treatment?"

"Dr. Abrams just didn't scare. He said if you wanted to call a full-scale Congressional investigation of his work with the Psi-Highs, and then serve him with a subpoena, he'll testify; otherwise, he said, you'd better stay off the Hoffman Center's back."

"Stubborn old goat," Ben Towne grumbled. "He knows I haven't got anything that would stand up in a Congressional probe." The secretary went back to the Sanders file, still tapping the floor with the cane. "Where *is* that Roberts? I can't wait here all day!"

The aide glanced down at Benjamin Towne with some curiosity. It was easy to see how the man had gained and held a Cabinet seat, and a powerful voice in the government, even though he opposed the President's views in regard to the training of Psi-High citizens. There was something overwhelming about his appearance—the heavy jaw and grim mouth line, the shock of sandy hair that fell over his forehead, the burning green eyes, the stout, well-muscled body. The aide's eyes drifted down to the man's withered left leg and the grotesque twisted foot, and he looked away in embarrassment. What was so awe-inspiring about a crippled man who accumulated great power? Towne certainly had done that. Some said that Ben Towne was the most powerful politician in the country since Senator Dan Fowler had died. Some even said that he was the greatest man, but that was something quite different indeed. And some said he was the most dangerous man in the Western Hemisphere, bar none. The aide shivered. That was none of his business. If he went probing *that* line too far, they'd be calling him Psi-High, and he liked his job too much to risk that.

The inner door opened, and a tall man with prematurely grey hair strode in, followed by a girl in her early twenties. "Sorry to hold you up, Mr. Secretary," the man said. "No, no, don't get up—we can talk right here."

Towne had made no effort to rise. He glared at the Federal Security chief, and then his eyes drifted angrily to the girl. "I said I wanted a *private* conference, Roberts. I don't want one of these brain-picking snoopers in the same room with me."

Bob Roberts shook his head as the girl turned to leave. "Sit down, Jean. Mr. Secretary, this is Jean Sanders. If you want to talk to me about the search for this alien, I want her to sit in."

Ben Towne slowly set the papers down on the floor. "Record this, if you please," he said to his aide. His eyes turned to Roberts. "I understand the alien slipped out of your hands again yesterday," he said with vicious smoothness. "A pity."

Roberts reddened. "That's right. He slipped away clean."

"No pictures, no identifications, no nothing, eh?"

"I'm afraid not."

Towne's voice was deadly. "Mr. Roberts, we both know that an unidentified creature totally alien to this planet made a landing three weeks ago and has been at large in this country, completely at large, ever since, and your Federal Security people haven't even gotten near him. I want to know why."

"I'd suggest that if you read our reports—"

"Look, man, I didn't come here for insolence!" Towne slammed the cane down with a clatter. "You're answerable to the Congress and Cabinet of the North American States for every wretched thing you do, and I'm ready to bring charges of criminal negligence against you in this alien investigation."

"Criminal negligence!" The Security chief stared at him. "Mr. Secretary, we've thrown everything we have into this search. The creature has played us for fools, every step of the way! We didn't even get a look at his ship; it blew up right in our faces! Do you realize what we're fighting here?"

"I realize quite well," said Towne, frostily. "You're fighting an alien creature who has slipped into our population, somehow, and just vanished. There's no guessing why he's here, what he wants, or what he's doing; there's no guessing anything about him, what powers he might have, what nature of beast he might be, or anything else. The very fact that he has sneaked in like a thief in the night suggests that his intentions are not benign, and until he is caught and interrogated, somehow, the potential threat of his presence is simply staggering. So what have you guardians of the nation done? For three weeks you've fumbled and alibied without even turning up a warm trail. You don't even have a coherent description of him."

"We're fighting a telepath," Roberts said softly. "An alien with telepathic powers such as we've never dreamed of. That's what we're fighting. And we're not winning, either."

The girl across the room stirred uneasily. Ben Towne's green eyes shot over to her viciously. "And you're using freaks like her to help hunt for him, I suppose. Or to help hide him, for all I know. If he's a telepath, then he's one of *their* kind."

"Jean Sanders is not a freak," Roberts said coldly. "She's an ordinary, intelligent human being who happens to have been born with a certain rudimentary degree of extrasensory perception which makes her Psi-High according to the Jim Crow laws you railroaded through Congress a few years ago. She's had intensive Hoffman Center training to help her develop her psi-potential, in spite of your efforts to get that training program killed. She is also a loyal citizen, and when it comes to tracking down and trapping a telepathic alien, she's about the most valuable asset we've got at the present moment. If not the *only* one. I just wish there were more Psi-Highs around with the training she's had."

Benjamin Towne glanced at his aide in triumph. "So! You openly *admit* that you've been using Psi-Highs in an investigation as critical as this!"

"Of course I have, to some extent! How do you think—"

"Then you're admitting criminal negligence right there, as far as I'm concerned," Towne cut him off.

Roberts sighed in disgust. "Mr. Towne, you don't have any idea what you're saying."

"I beg to differ," Towne said with heat. "I happen to believe that there are a group of individuals wandering around loose who will have the rest of this country in chains in a hundred years if they're allowed to develop and use their freak powers the way they want to. Psi-Highs are a vicious menace, nothing more or less. We can't help it that we have them; the fools in the government two hundred years ago must have been blind when they first started turning up, but nobody realized then that the psi-factor was a straight Mendelian dominant inheritable trait, and by the time we found that out it was too late to have them all sterilized. Of course, they couldn't use their extrasensory powers without special training, so even then drastic measures didn't seem necessary." He picked up his cane and leaned forward toward Roberts. "Didn't *seem* necessary, that is. But now the good Dr. Reuben Abrams and his meddling crowd at the Hoffman Center are busy training them, teaching some of them to *use* their psi-faculties, providing them with a treacherous power that has no place in civilized society. Well, I'm going to get that stopped, don't worry. And meanwhile, *I don't want them working in Security!* Is that clear enough?"

Roberts sighed tiredly, and leaned back in his chair. "You're a little confused, Mr. Secretary. This is not a Rotary Club luncheon. It's not a Federal Isolationist rally, and it's not a meeting of the Cabinet. It's just me you're talking to. And so far, to my knowledge, you haven't succeeded in robbing Psi-High citizens of *all* their rights. You've passed laws forcing them to take psychiatric tests and submit to Federal registration, just like drug addicts. They have to report to your Medical Affairs Department underlings every month like paroled convicts. You've passed laws to prevent them from marrying, you've blocked their education and hamstrung their training and development, you've done your level best to poison the minds of the general psi-negative public against them, but you haven't, as yet, been able to strip them of their citizenship."

"Not as yet," said Ben Towne.

"And you can't, as yet, dictate to me how I am to run the activities of the Federal Security Commission."

"Not as yet."

Roberts' eyes blazed. "All right. Now you listen carefully, Mr. Secretary, tape recording or no tape recording. We've got an enemy in our midst, an alien we've never even seen. That alien *could* be the most malignant threat we've ever faced in all history. We can thank a psi-positive citizen out in Des Moines, Iowa, that we ever discovered the alien was here at all. That citizen had the good sense and the loyalty to report to us when he had accidental extrasensory contact with a psi-presence stronger than any he had ever encountered before, and thought that this was very strange. Normal psi-negative individuals can't recognize this alien for what he is, can't identify him, can't even get near him. We know that because we've tried. So far we have *not* used Psi-High agents against him, but we're going to have to, whether you happen to like it or not. Psi-negatives are whipped, the alien can run circles around them. Our only hope of catching him is to fight fire with fire, and in this case the only fire we have is the best-trained psi-positive agents we can get our hands on. Like Jean Sanders here. Or Ted Marino in Chicago. So that's the way it is. You can try to stop me if you want to, but you're going to have to reorganize Federal Security to do it."

Benjamin Towne lurched to his feet, his face white. "I may do that, Roberts." He reached for his cane. "I may just do that."

"Then you'll have to throw the Liberal Administration out of office first. They're supporting me, and they're outvoting the Isolationists two to one. The President is also supporting me."

Towne gave him a shrewd look. "Well, you'd better start watching the telecasts and newstapes," he said bluntly. "There are already rumors going around about some kind of a mysterious alien fugitive—oh, I know it's been classified top secret, but you know how secrets leak out." He grinned maliciously. "People get nervous about rumors like that, especially when the Administration denies them so sharply. You'd just better catch that alien pretty fast, that's my advice." The secretary nodded to his aide and limped to the door. Then he glanced back over his shoulder. "And if you're *really* smart, you'll keep your Psi-High freaks out of it, or you're going to wish you'd never heard of them before."

The door slammed behind him. Jean Sanders stood up, white-faced and trembling. "What a vicious man," she murmured. "What did he mean, Bob? About wishing you'd never heard of us?"

Robert Roberts shook his head slowly. "I'm not sure I know," he said.

3

PAUL FAIRCLOTH finished reading the teletape briefing just as the little jet helicopter slipped down toward the hangar slot in South Chicago. He tossed the spools into the erasure can and flipped the switch to activate the distortion field inside the can. Then he stretched his legs, so tense he could hardly move them, and stared out at the city rising up below. For the twentieth time he wondered if he was going to come out of this alien mess alive or not, and for the twentieth time he wished it were all over.

It wasn't all over, of course. Down there somewhere in that city, in a room high in a residential skyscraper, an utterly imponderable and dangerous alien creature from another world was once more located and pinpointed in a specific area at a specific time. It was Paul Faircloth's job, now, to see that he did not again break through the dragnet.

Jean's parting hug was still warm in his memory, and he

remembered the worry in her big grey eyes as she had kissed him and said, "Be careful, Paul. I wish I could go, too. I don't know what I'd do if anything happened—" Only words, spoken aloud, but she had said so much, much more without words. Those unspoken things were only vague shadows in Paul Faircloth's mind, but even so he could sense the meaning of those shadows.

A man was waiting for him down below on the landing ramp. The hangar vault was dark and deserted, probably Security's work, too, he thought. He scanned the agent's ID card, even though the face was familiar enough. "Marino? I'm Paul Faircloth. Where do we stand?"

"No change since you left Washington," Marino said. "He's still there." The agent was a small, wiry man with catlike movements and exceedingly bright eyes under his jet black eyebrows. "We'd better be on our way over while I brief you."

Faircloth nodded, and stepped into the little tube-car waiting at the end of the platform. It was a tight fit for two men, and Paul stiffened by reflex as it lurched and dipped down the chute into a narrow tunnel, hanging from the overhead cable and speeding ahead on its electronic guide beam. "You said it was the Condor Building where he was spotted?"

Marino nodded. "In Center City Chicago. First thirty-six floors are commercial, and the twenty above are residential. You've studied the floor plan? Fine. He's pretty definitely holed up in a large residential suite on the forty-second floor. No guessing why he chose it, or how long he's been there, but I'm one hundred percent certain that that's where he is—" He shot Faircloth a nervous glance, almost apologetic. "I'm Psi-High, you know. That's why I'm sure he's there. I located him and then three of us got him triangulated. Hard to explain exactly *how*, but we did, and we can keep him pinned pretty well, too. If he doesn't try to shower us, that is. We're pretty sure he knows we're there."

"What do you mean, shower you?"

Marino tapped his forehead grimly. "Throw a barrage at us, the works. This creature has powerful voltage, and I mean *powerful*. He showered one of our Psi-High people yesterday, and it was brutal. Nearly ripped his mind apart."

Faircloth shivered. "But you can keep track of him."

"Yes." Marino lit a cigarette with nervous fingers. "Whether *you* can or not is something else again. No offense. I know it's a touchy thing, but it's just plain fact that psi-negatives have trouble keeping track of this bird at all without the help of psi-contact. You really shouldn't be here at all, as far as logic is concerned, but those are the orders. Roberts put us Psi-Highs out to spot him, but he doesn't want any Psi-Highs in on the kill." Marino's voice was flat with disappointment. "Political pressure, I guess. Wouldn't do to give a Psi-High credit for anything." He glanced at Faircloth and reddened. "Sorry, it just slipped out." He bit his lip. "Anyway, you're to have a dozen other psi-negatives to help you. I hope God'll be helping you too."

Faircloth grinned tightly. "Got you nervous?"

"It's got me plenty nervous."

"Well, cheer up. Those 'orders' were strictly for the record that Benjamin Towne is going to be seeing sooner or later. Roberts has no intention of pulling you off this, or any of the others, Psi-High or otherwise. As for me, I want your best Psi-High men—every one of them—to go in with me. We've got to *get* this creature, and get him cold. He's slick, and he's too dangerous to fool around with. Have you got the building sewed up?"

Marino grinned. "Tight as a vacuum."

"Good. Keep it very unobstrusive and try to keep the Psi-Highs from broadcasting any more than they have to."

Marino gave him a queer look. "They'll do the best they can, of course."

"Right." Faircloth ran a hand through his brown hair, and loosened his tie a trifle. "As soon as rush hour is over and the building is cleared we'll go up in the elevator. I want the power cut the second we step off, all over the building. Elevators, lights, everything. We'll be on the forty-first floor, and we'll have a team on the forty-third. Then we'll close in together. Sound all right?"

Marino shrugged. "I guess so. Thing is, they had him boxed in just as tight in Des Moines last week and he slid right through." The man's eyes were worried. "We just don't know what we're fighting. That's the whole trouble. Even the Psi-Highs are up a tree."

The car gave a lurch, and slid to a stop. They stepped out into a brightly lighted tunnel filled with people emptying out of the huge building above. The two men waited to board an express surface elevator, and stepped off on the main concourse of the Condor Building. The last sunset rays made a dazzling golden display on the banks of heliomirrors, and Faircloth blinked, shielding his eyes a moment after the softer light below. Then he glanced at his watch. "Let's get some coffee," he said. "We've got a few minutes."

They slid into an eating booth along the concourse and dropped in coins for coffee. It was so clumsy, this whole approach, Faircloth thought. Three and a half weeks since the ship had been spotted along the Mississippi, and they were still just learning how clumsy they were. Right from the beginning, when the first report of alien contact had come in, and the ship itself discovered, the attempt to examine it was a blunder. Even a crack demolition team couldn't get near it. It had exploded when they were ten yards away. And then picking up the alien's trail—true, they had been able to trace his route from the first farmhouse where he had stopped the night he landed, then west through the farm country to Des Moines, then northeast to the great Chicago metropolis. But when it came to contacting the creature, or capturing him . . . Faircloth shook his head. Clumsy just wasn't the right word.

He glanced at Marino, and reached across the booth and buzzed for a newstape. He scanned the Washington news hurriedly—another upheaval in the Liberal Party over the Coalition question with South America—another proposed International Joint Council meeting—and another vicious attack by Medical Affairs Secretary Benjamin Towne on the Hoffman Center's training program for Psi-Highs. Denouncing Dr. Reuben Abrams as the leader in a plan to train all Psi-High deviants (Towne actually used the word!) and to seek repeal of the present laws preventing two Psi-Highs from marrying. Paul went tense, searching for Jean Sanders' name. It was not mentioned, and he took a deep breath and clenched his fist. If that filthy rabble rouser ever dragged her name into the public eye— He finished his coffee, watching sourly as the tape moved slowly up the screen.

Then his eye caught a small item with a Des Moines dateline, well hidden among the minor items. He read it, frowning:

Woman Charges Psi-High Conspiracy

Des Moines, Ia., 27 June, 2177. A woman whose name was withheld today placed charges of assault and invasion of privacy against Miss Martha Bishop, 23, of Oak Park Section, Chicago, whose name is listed in the Federal psi-positive registry. The charge, made at local Federal Security offices, accused Miss Bishop of gross mental interference. The victim, who allegedly had information concerning "rumors of an alien visitor" claimed that Miss Bishop had attempted to prevent her from reporting her information to authorities. After failing in this attempt, Miss Bishop allegedly employed her psi-powers to erase the information from the woman's mind. Miss Bishop could not be reached for comment.

Mr. J. B. Dunlap, Liberal Administration spokesman, has repeatedly denied other rumors of alien visitors which have been persistently appearing this summer. Nevertheless, the charges against Miss Bishop are being investigated fully—

Faircloth snapped off the tape angrily and returned to his coffee. Finally he nodded to Marino. "Better drink up," he said, "and contact your men. It's time to go."

Marino finished his coffee in a gulp. Then they stepped out onto the concourse again.

4

TED MARINO left to give his men a final briefing, arranging to meet Faircloth back in the concourse five minutes later. Paul found a visiphone relay booth, and sank his long, lean body down in a relaxer facing the screen. The last of the rush hour people were still drifting by in the corridor; Paul watched them anxiously. If only he could talk to Jean! He wondered what she would think of the news item from Des Moines. He battled an impulse to call her, then compromised and dialed the priority code for the Federal Security Commission offices in Washington.

The relays clicked, and the code carried him through the front-line secretaries without any trouble. He gave a sigh of relief. He was in no mood to argue with secretaries. A moment later he was blinking at Roberts' 3-D image on the screen.

Roberts' face, usually quite youthful in sharp contrast to

his grey hair, looked haggard now. He nodded to Faircloth. "You got there, then. Good. How does it look, Paul?"

"Everything's just real nice," Faircloth growled. "They think they've got him pinned. I hope so. The building here has a central power source, and we can bottleneck the whole place if we time it right."

"Don't miss, Paul." Roberts' voice was tense. "Whatever you do, don't miss."

"What's the matter?"

"Ben Towne has worked his way into this."

"Well, that figures. But what can he do?"

"Maybe a lot, if we miss this time. He has the whole Isolationist Party behind him, and the Liberals can't hold out long on no results. Towne has a whole lot of people worried about these alien rumors, and if we don't wrap it up fast I'm afraid things here in the Capitol are going to blow sky high."

Faircloth scowled. "Did you see the newstapes tonight?"

"You mean the Bishop girl in Des Moines?" Roberts nodded unhappily. "Got the report from Des Moines on it this afternoon. Trumped up from beginning to end. I tell you, Towne is not playing around. I don't know just how he plans to work things, but I'm afraid that story was just a starter. He'll do everything he can to spread the rumor without an outright Security leak, and he'll do his best to connect the alien with the Psi-Highs in the public eye. And you know Ben Towne when he gets rolling. The way things are in the Senate now, that could mean real trouble."

"Who's controlling Security news releases?"

Roberts gave a short laugh. "I am, of course. But they're monitored by the Cabinet, and Towne is on the Cabinet. Don't miss tonight, my friend."

Faircloth nodded, and signaled off. He sat swearing quietly to himself for a few moments. Then he saw Marino and swung out into the hall again, glancing at his watch. "Ready?"

Marino nodded. "I've got teams placed on the forty-first and forty-third. Power goes off when we step off the elevator on the forty-first. Okay?"

Faircloth grunted, and spread out a floor plan of the Forty-second floor, studying the careful pencil marks. "Is the building all clear?"

"The commercial levels, yes. And autolocks go on every door in the place but the one we want when the power goes off."

"Good. At least we won't have residents underfoot. You've got Psi-Highs posted outside the building?"

"Yes, in 'copters. Circling the building fairly close, out of sight range of the forty-second."

"All right. We'll move in on him as soon as the power goes off. I want cameras going everywhere—in the corridors, in the stairwells, even in the 'copters outside. We're going to get him, but in case somehow we don't I want to see where he goes, and especially I want to get a picture of him. A *good* picture of him. Maybe he can fuzz up human eyesight, but he'll have trouble fuzzing up a photo plate. Let's go."

They stepped on the elevator, felt it rush up until the automatic brake slowed it and stopped at the forty-first floor. They stepped off. As the door closed behind them, the whirring motors died, and the lights went out. Faircloth led the way swiftly to the closed stairwell where they met four other men standing by, one with a motion camera. "Cover everything," Paul said sharply. "If you see him, stop him with a shocker, *not* with pellets. We want him alive." He opened the stairwell and started up with the men behind him. Moments later they met part of the group from the forty-third; they started swiftly down the dark corridor toward the pinpointed residential suite—

And then, like a bolt of lightning, something exploded in Faircloth's brain. He cried out, felt his arms jerk, and fell forward on his face. Wave after wave of blinding light seemed to burn through his brain; he couldn't see, couldn't move, couldn't even force a sound from his throat. Somewhere nearby he heard shouts, and a whistle shrilled. Someone was running, and someone else tripped over him, tumbling to the floor with a bone-jarring crash. He tried to move, tried to fight the blinding, searing waves of fire in his mind, like staring into a succession of flashbulbs going off *whoom—whoom—whoom* right before his eyes, but nothing worked right. Three shots rang out even as he dragged himself to his knees, controlling his rebellious muscles by sheer force of willpower. Blinded, he clawed his way along the wall as more footsteps echoed frantically in the corridor. Suddenly, Marino was shaking his arm, helping him up, and together they pushed aside the open door of the target suite as a roar of malignant, derisive laughter seemed to burst and echo and re-echo in his mind. . . .

Faircloth opened his eyes. Through a burning red haze of pain, he saw the empty room. Then his legs gave way and he collapsed on a chair, exhausted, as Marino raced from room to room like a madman.

"Gone," Marino groaned.

Unbelieving, Faircloth stared at him. "You—you got him on the stairs, didn't you?"

Marino shook his head miserably. "Nobody could see him. Not a soul. He hit us with a shower and that was that. Must have gone down that stairwell like a shot, and if we didn't get him, nobody stopped him below either."

"What about the cameras?" Faircloth gasped.

"Three of them are smashed. I don't know about the rest."

"You're *certain?*"

Marino didn't answer. The answer was obvious. The alien had struck once, and slipped away from them like a ghost in the night.

5

ROBERT ROBERTS was waiting, nervous as a cat, when Faircloth arrived at the Security office. There were deep circles under his pale grey eyes, and a dark stubble on his chin. He greeted Paul with a silent handshake; then they went back into the rear office, with its modern paneled wall looking out across the valley to the tall white buildings of the Capitol. Once it had been an inspiring sight to Faircloth. Now he hardly even noticed. A rocket rose in the morning air, leaving its white vapor trail like a pillar of cloud behind it. The weekly Venus rocket, probably, or maybe one of the dozens of speculator ships off for Titan. Faircloth scowled and sank into a relaxer with a sigh. "I'm sorry, Bob," he said. "It was a bust. I thought we had him cold, and we weren't even near him."

Roberts mixed a drink and shoved it across the desk to Paul. "Okay, sometimes we don't win. What we've got to know is *why* you weren't even near him. Something went sour. What was it?"

Faircloth was silent for a long moment. Then he said: "Bob —you're not going to like this."

"What do you mean?"

"I mean I think it's more than this one fiasco in Chicago. I think our whole approach is sour from one end to the other. I think it has been from the beginning. And unless we try something radically different, I don't think we're going to get this bird, *ever.*"

"But what's *wrong* with the approach?" Roberts asked.

"We're outclassed, that's what's wrong with it. This alien is out of our league—way out. We haven't got a thing that can touch him, and he knows it. He's a *telepath*, Bob, and I don't mean halfway. Not just a feeble, groping, half-baked, half-trained, poorly developed Psi-High human. We're dealing with telepathic power no human Psi-High ever began to approach."

Roberts' lips were tight. "Exactly what *did* happen in Chicago?"

"That's just it. I don't know. The building was virtually escape-proof. The boys had every exit guarded three ways from Sunday. The power was off in the entire building, and there was *no* way he could get out short of walking through walls. And we had the walls guarded just in case he did that. We had him sewed up beyond hope of escape, and then when we went in to get him, *whammo!*" Faircloth clenched his fists, trembling. "I don't want to go through that again, Bob, *not for anything*. It was murderous. He hit one of the boys so hard that it's going to take the psych-docs six months to get his brain unscrambled. I got off easy. All he handed me was a sort of gentle rap on the knuckles."

"And he slid through your net."

"Clean. As far as I know he just walked out and hailed a taxi. Believe me, all *I* was trying to do was merely get up off the floor. He smashed the cameras and got away without leaving a trace."

Roberts shook his head and fished a folder from his desk. "He didn't smash *all* the cameras." He shoved the pictures across to Paul. "See what you make of those."

Faircloth peered at them. There were several frames, obviously printed from motion-film. Pictures of a humanoid figure running down a passageway. The face was not visible. "Not much help," he said. "Not even for a clothing description. Can't even be sure it isn't one of our men."

Roberts sighed. "I know. And you didn't see him at all?"

Faircloth shook his head. "As I said, the whole approach is sour. We're *never* going to get him this way."

"Then I hope you've got some different ideas."

"I have."

"Well, I'm glad somebody has." Some of the tiredness left Roberts' face. "Let's have them."

Paul Faircloth looked at the Security chief and shook his head. "Sorry," he said. "First I want some answers, straight answers about a certain individual."

"You mean Ben Towne."

"That's right."

Roberts scowled. "All right, I'll tell you about Ben Towne. It isn't pretty. Frankly, this Chicago business was the break Towne has been waiting for. There were Psi-Highs involved in that raid. Towne knows it. And he's going to build a story of Psi-High alliance with the alien that could get every Psi-High in the country thrown into prison and *might* even put Ben Towne in political control of the country."

Faircloth nodded grimly. "Does he have any concept of how dangerous this creature is?"

Roberts snorted. "Of course he has! But Ben Towne is obsessed with a single idea, and it twists and distorts everything else in his mind." He leaned forward, staring at Paul. "Benjamin Towne wants to wipe psi-positive faculties off the face of the Earth. He hates Psi-Highs. Oh, I don't know the motives behind it—maybe the fact of his own imperfect body makes him hate what he considers a sort of super-perfection appearing in the human race. It's a false premise, of course. The predisposition of certain people to extrasensory powers is neither a perfection nor an imperfection; it's a quality their minds happen to have. Just another tiny step in the evolutionary chain, and it isn't all fun and games for them either. It isn't any fun for a woman like Jean Sanders to have to be gratuitously assaulted, day after day, by all the rot flowing out of some of the cesspool minds we have walking the streets. That's part of the price *she* has to pay for her precious gift, and for her special training. She can't turn it off too well, any more. Well, it happens to be a dominant gene factor, and in *our society* it happens to put the Psi-High in a slightly advantageous position in comparison to psi-negatives." Roberts threw up his hands. "But Benjamin Towne's motives don't really matter. He was smart enough to realize that there were lots of people who hated and feared the expansion of Psi-High powers in our society. He started fighting against it, and he's ridden that fight right into the Cabinet. Already he's got the Psi-Highs marked and hamstrung. His next goal is to block any training for them, even if it means destroying the Hoffman Medical Center in order to do it."

"But they're only *doctors*," Faircloth protested.

"Not quite; they're more than doctors. They're *researchers* in a vast, government supported complex, looking for answers to questions about what human beings are and what they can do. They're probing everywhere—in medicine, in biochemistry, in physiology, in psychiatry. And like researchers in other areas of science, they haven't been overconcerned about whether what they learned was *good* for people or *bad* for people. They have simply been concerned to find out *what human beings are capable of*."

"Well—is this *bad?*"

"Not necessarily—nor good, either," Roberts said. "The Hoffman Center idea has never been massively popular; they've always been under attack from one quarter or another, and some of the things they've done have surely not been *good*. There was the big scandal about the Mercy Men, 'way back when the center was very new. Hiring bums and derelicts from Skid Roads and Front Streets all over the country as medical mercenaries, to serve as human guinea pigs was good business for research, I guess, but so repugnant to most people that it was finally outlawed by Congress. And take the rejuvenation program—Senator Dan Fowler found the flaw in that, and

Carl Golden got it stopped for good when he won his Senate seat. Oh, they still use the techniques, all right, rebuilding bodies torn to pieces in auto accidents, prolonging productive lives for a few years, fighting back incurable diseases. But mass-rejuvenation turned out to be meddling—*bad* meddling—with natural processes that had a purpose to them, and so it was stopped."

There was silence for a moment. Paul Faircloth took a deep breath. "And do you think that training Psi-Highs is also bad?"

"Of course I don't, but Ben Towne does."

"And where does the alien fit in this picture?"

Roberts shrugged. "It's obvious, isn't it? Towne has taken an issue and split the country wide open with it. And now, along comes a visitor from the stars, an alien visitor who steps out of his ship and disappears into the population like a spirit. An alien who is *fully telepathic*. Towne can monitor the news releases, he can even help decide on the security classification of information about the alien. It's been kept top secret, so far. But Ben can control the news enough to tie Psi-High humans and a fearfully dangerous enemy alien together so neatly in the public mind that every Psi-High in the country will be in danger of his life. It's political dynamite, and Towne is controlling the fuse."

Faircloth's face was white. "And if the alien is caught?"

"At this point, it's very touchy. It *might* be that the 'rumored' liaison between Psi-High humans and invaders from space could be 'proved.' And then Towne would be in the driver's seat."

Faircloth nodded bitterly, and stood up, shaking the creases out of his trousers. His face was grim. As he reached for his hat, his hand was trembling. "That's just about the way I had it lined up, too," he said. "So long, Bob. Have a nice hunt."

"Sit down, Paul."

"Sorry. I'm not working to help Ben Towne."

"No, but you're going to work to fight him," Roberts snapped. He sat up straight behind the desk. "You're going to work with me, my friend, and you're going to follow through to the bitter end. You and Jean both."

Faircloth's eyes darkened. "Jean's not involved in this."

"I am afraid she is. Just as deeply as you are. And you and Jean are going to do what I tell you to do in this investigation whether you happen to like it or not. That is, if you ever want to marry her."

Faircloth turned slowly. "What do you mean by that? What are you saying?"

"I'm saying that you happen to be Psi-High, Paul. And I just happen to know it."

6   PAUL FAIRCLOTH sank down in the chair again, staring at Roberts in silence. Then he said: "That's a pretty bad joke, Bob."

Roberts nodded. "I'll say it's a joke. It's a colossal horse-laugh on Ben Towne. He was so dead certain that those Federal registry files of his contained the names and life histories of every psi-positive individual in the country! It's no joke as far as you're concerned, though. It's against Federal law to forge psycho-testing papers, Paul. It's against the law for a Psi-High to remain unregistered, and in the rare cases that have turned up the courts haven't exactly been lenient. It's also against the law for two Psi-Highs to marry; the law's attitude is that having people around with a single dominant gene is bad enough without doubling them up, and *that* law is enforced to the limit, regardless of how well or poorly the psi-powers are developed in the individuals involved. Of course, Jean's work with Dr. Abrams at the Hoffman Center has developed her powers amazingly. Yours must be pretty crude for you to keep them hidden so well."

"You can't prove a thing you're saying," Faircloth said.

"True enough—nothing substantial. Just a few curiosities in your history that caught my eye, and then a little quiet personal investigation. You were already out of school when the registry law was passed, and you must have gotten somebody to leak the examination to you early. How you did it, I neither know nor care. But the law provides for compulsory retesting any time anyone raises a reasonable doubt." He smiled at Faircloth cheerfully. "Care to have me call Dr. Abrams? He's got some nice definitive tests."

Faircloth's eyes fell. "That won't be necessary." He sighed and sank wearily back into the relaxer. "I guess I knew I'd be spotted sooner or later. I even thought for a while that Marino had spotted it."

"He did."

"But I never thought you'd be the one to crowd me."

Roberts looked up at him. "Paul, I'm not fighting you. Matter of fact, I'm not even threatening you nor telling you what you have to do. I'm not going to call the law on you; it's a vicious law that I hate as much as you do, even though I have the job of implementing it. If you want to walk out on me and this investigation right now, you can do it and I won't lift a finger against you. All I'm really doing is asking you not to walk out."

"What do you want me to do?"

"I want you to work with me until this alien is caught. I think we can nail him, and I think we can sink Benjamin Towne's boat at the same time. I'm convinced that there's no single human being in the country as dangerous to Ben Towne and his ambitions as an unregistered, unidentified Psi-High. And that's just what you are. With you and Jean working as a team, I think we can wrap up this alien hunt and turn it to the advantage of every Psi-High in the country."

Faircloth shook his head, puzzled. "I don't follow you."

"Are you blind? Think for a minute. If one telepathic alien has made a landing on this planet, *don't you suppose others are going to follow?* And if they do—suppose they mount a massive invasion—*who do you think is going to stop them?*"

The light broke, and Faircloth nodded. "Of course. I was just so wrapped up in my own problems that I never thought— but you're right."

"Okay, you said you had some ideas. Let's have them."

"They may not be any good," Paul said. "And it would take Jean to put them across."

"Jean is willing. She's been reading this whole conversation from the next room."

"Then let's get her in here and do some planning. The first job we have is to pin down this alien and *keep* him pinned."

7

HOURS LATER Jean Sanders tossed her pencil on the desk, and flopped down cross-legged on the floor. "I think we're going around in circles," she said in disgust. "Three different circles," she added, with an owlish glance at Bob Roberts.

"All right, I know we're tired." The Security chief sighed.

"But the answer is *here,* somewhere," Faircloth said doggedly. "It's *got* to be here! We have all the data we need, if we could only pinpoint some way to use it. Or at least we've got enough data to make a start."

"The more I think about this whole business," the girl said, "the more fishy it looks." She was a pretty girl, with a slender face, black brows, and huge grey eyes. She was twenty-three, but her slim figure made her look sixteen. "From what we know about this alien and what he *could* do, what we know that he's actually *done* doesn't make any sense at all. It gets fishier and fishier the more we talk about it."

Paul nodded. "Exactly. There's something that we aren't seeing or realizing, or something important that we just don't know about this creature."

"Well, let's see what we do know," said Roberts. "We've got a photograph that isn't worth a plugged nickel. We've got a few photos of the outside of the ship before it exploded. We know that he's Psi-Triple-High, fully telepathic, and able to muddle up the minds of all who see him so they can't describe him."

"Or can't see that anything's wrong about him," Jean added. "He *must* have a disguise. Maybe it isn't perfect enough. Maybe he has to work constantly with his mind to hide all the little flaws."

Faircloth walked across the room, staring at the walls. "Then there's the matter of the ship. It was found near Gutenberg, Iowa, on a bluff overlooking the Mississippi, over a month ago. That's a fact. Some farm kids found it, but didn't go near it. Scared stiff. Told their father, and he called the police, and they called Security. I don't suppose there was any way to tell how long the ship had been there *before* it was found?"

Roberts shook his head. "The biologists and geologists both had a whack at it, but the explosion destroyed all the flora around it and tore up the ground area within twenty feet of it. Nothing left to study. Well, anyway, no occupant of the ship was found, and no trace of where the occupant might have gone; at least, not then. Security sent a scout squad down to photograph the ship and try to examine it, and it blew into a million pieces right in their faces."

"How many of the million pieces were recovered?" Faircloth asked.

"About ten. Fragments of aluminum alloy, completely twisted and distorted. Told us nothing."

Faircloth nodded. "Okay. Then there was the report from the Psi-High in Des Moines, and you turned up the farmer and his wife who saw the alien the first night. What was their name? Bettendorf, Jacob Bettendorf. Not very bright folks, I gather. They fed him, but refused him lodging and sent him on his way. Noticed nothing odd, except that the farmer said his eyes felt tired all the time the creature was there, couldn't seem to focus right. How did his description compare with the others you've gotten?"

Roberts shrugged. "The same, or I should say, consistently different. Nobody seems to agree on *anything*. It's obvious that nobody has *actually* seen him in any detail at all. People just think they have."

"You know," said the girl suddenly, "that's one of the things that bothers me. A lot of those people out there are Ben Towne's strongest supporters. They don't like Psi-Highs. They keep watching like hawks for people who act like Psi-Highs— you know, the way we're likely to nod and start answering a question before a person gets it half asked; or the way we sometimes forget to control our expressions when somebody is saying one thing out loud and thinking something directly the opposite. People spot that, and get very indignant at being caught red-handed. Snooping, they call it. But this alien went right past them. Not even a suspicion."

"He got into the city fast, though," Roberts observed. "City people tend to be a lot less observant of others around them than country folks."

"All right," said Paul. "That fits well enough. Now, since he was willing to destroy his ship, we can assume that he planned to stay a while. That probably means that others were here before him. He's just altogether too confident for any advance scout. He *knew* he could mingle with people, and stay here, and observe, and learn, and get away with it. Probably his job is to accumulate information, detailed information about human beings. Well, with full-blown telepathy working for him, he must really be having a time for himself! And unless I miss my guess, the information he wants most of all is *information about Psi-Highs.*"

Roberts shrugged. "Okay, I agree. But what does this add up to?"

Faircloth looked at him grimly. "Seems to me it adds up to one thing: *we aren't going to catch him in any dragnet.* No matter how skillfully we lay it out. No matter how many Psi-Highs we have in on it, and no matter how well trained they are."

"Then you're saying that we aren't going to get him, period."

"Not quite. I think we *can* catch him if we go at it the right way. At least we might have a chance, with a different approach. We'll have no way to evaluate it, at first, because of the nature of the approach, but in the end, we'll either have the alien or we won't, and I think there's a better than even chance that we will. If we keep playing the game we played in Chicago, we're going to lose every time."

"But what went wrong in Chicago?" Roberts cried.

"Nothing, except that we were whipped before we even started. Look at it this way. He's outguessed us, consistently, every time, right from the start. And it's not really surprising that he has. He doesn't need a three-hour briefing and a road map to tell what's going on around him. All he needs is a hint, the barest touch of a man's mind, the slightest flicker of contact, and he already has enough of a headstart to figure out everything that's going to happen from then on. Just like a chess game—you play along, and suddenly your opponent makes a move that reveals a whole complex gambit he's been pursuing that you hadn't even noticed before. But our alien friend spots the same gambit *before the first move* instead of after the tenth. We make a move, and he's already ahead of us. By now he knows human minds operate along fairly logical lines, he can figure out all the logical possibilities before they happen, and figure a defense for each possibility, and we just can't trap him, Psi-Highs or no Psi-Highs."

Roberts scowled at him. "Then what do you propose?"

Faircloth grinned. "That we change the ground rules on him without tipping him off. That we take all the evidence we have here, and feed it into a computer and let it meditate a while and plot out a supremely logical approach for us to follow in order to trap the creature on the basis of what we know about him now. Then we take that supremely logical approach and change it a bit. This creature is assuming we'll follow a logical approach. What we need is a supremely *illogical* approach."

8

THE CALL they were expecting came through at last, at three o'clock one morning after they had almost given it up in despair.

It had been a long, heartbreaking wait. Time after time Faircloth had argued that they must have been very close in Chicago, closer than they realized. The alien must actually have been frightened, he insisted, because since Chicago there had been no sign, no clue to his whereabouts, no hint that he was even in existence any more. Yet Faircloth was certain that the contact was bound to come, sooner or later.

It was possible, of course, that the change in the search pattern had worried the alien. Logically, a dragnet should have been set up in Chicago, and the entranceways to all the large cities guarded carefully. That was what the computer had said. "Probability is strong that the alien desires to remain in a city, but evidence suggests that Chicago may not be the optimum location for him. Recommend heavy Security measures be taken in all surrounding cities of size as well as Chicago. Probability is four-plus high that the alien is seeking some specific information. Advise close control of all spaceports, air transit outlets and rolling-road escapeways."

And so forth. That was what the computer had said. Of course, the computer was not infallible, but its analysis and recommendations were utterly logical on the basis of the information given it.

Which was exactly the reason they were being carefully ignored.

It was a gamble, and no one was more aware of this than Faircloth. Reluctantly, Roberts pulled all Security personnel *out* of the Chicago area, Psi-High and otherwise, except for a small crew headed by Ted Marino, who were scattered throughout the city with orders to carefully avoid contact among themselves. A gamble, but it was not entirely guesswork that made Paul so certain that the alien, if left suddenly and completely alone, would try to make contact with a Psi-High mind sooner or later. Of course, that conclusion itself was the result of logical reasoning. No matter *how* they tried to remove logic from their approach, it crept in, it *had* to creep in. It was logical that a telepathically sensitive creature, visiting an alien planet in obvious secrecy, would seek to learn something about the segment of the population that might be able to expose his presence. He would seek signs of his own kind of mental capability. He might even *have* to; Paul knew all too well that a Psi-High mind cut off and isolated from any psi-contact soon was a sick mind. That was why Psi-Highs always settled in the cities, why they sought each other out with such fierce, desperate clannishness—a tendency which, in itself, had bred suspicion of Psi-Highs in the minds of psi-negatives. What psi-negatives couldn't really comprehend was that with Psi-Highs *it wasn't a matter of choice*. It was a desperate need. And Paul knew how overwhelming that need could be.

No, logically the alien would make contact with a human Psi-High, sooner or later. It would not be difficult to spot such a contact. The Psi-Highs were very few in number, only a couple of hundred scattered in small colonies in the larger cities of the North American States. With painstaking care each one had been contacted and warned, and those working in Security were staked out in the most likely places for the contact that they expected. The roads were left free, and the airports and spaceports were not checked. No dragnet—just an invisible network of human minds spread across the country, delicately tuned, waiting for the spark of contact.

Faircloth was asleep when the call finally came. He rolled groggily out of bed and snapped on the visiphone screen. Ted Marino's face materialized eerily, a frightened, shaking Marino whose eyes were wide with horror, and whose hands jerked and jerked as he tried to control them. His voice was on the thin edge of hysteria. "He hit me, Paul. Just a little while ago. He hit me hard."

Paul leaned forward, staring at the man's face. He had expected contact. He had not expected *this* kind of contact. "Ted, are you hurt?"

"No, no. But let me tell you, I can't take that again."

"You're sure it wasn't just another Psi-High contacting you? It's deadly important, Ted."

Marino shook his head vehemently. "No, no, no. It *couldn't* have been that. I know what normal Psi-High contact is like. This was—different. It was as if he'd opened up my skull and scooped out my brains."

Faircloth nodded, trembling with excitement. "Did you try to fight him?"

"I tried. He had me wide open before I knew what had happened, but I tried. I—I think it *puzzled* him. It didn't stop him at all, he just brushed it aside like cobwebs, but it puzzled him—" The man hesitated. "It was awful, Paul. I want to get this bird as badly as you, but I don't know if I can stand another blast like that."

"You aren't going to have to," Faircloth said. "You've done great, but your part in it is over now. Don't write a report about what happened. Don't even think about it. Get dressed and get on a plane out of there. Go to Florida, Rio, any place as long as it's remote and out of touch. Use your expense account, and have yourself the time of your life."

Marino's eyes opened in amazement. "Are you crazy? I thought this was what we've been waiting for!"

"It is, but your part in the plan is over. Do what I say and don't worry about it. When you've gotten a good rest, come back to the Hoffman Center and take up your training with Dr. Abrams where you left off." Paul flipped the switch, and turned back to the room, exultant. He clapped his hands in glee, and began to pack his bag.

The chase was on, with a vengeance. But this time, the mouse was chasing the cat.

9

THEN, AS if a dam had broken, the reports began streaming in. Three more came from Chicago, one from Cleveland, from a Psi-High technician there who was not even remotely connected with Security. From Pittsburgh, from New Philadelphia. Like a fearful, ominous flood, reports of the alien's contacts swarmed in. Paul Faircloth and Jean Sanders plotted them, and waited, and got ready.

Their headquarters were in a small suite of rooms in a middle class residential hotel in the heavily built-up metropolitan area between Washington and Baltimore. Few Federal Security agents, Psi-High or otherwise, knew this; all most of the team had was a visiphone priority code number, and a special word-key for scrambling messages. Faircloth had insisted on this. Of all the agents posted and assigned, only Paul, Jean, and Roberts knew the true nature of the operation. Each of them worked out his own illogical details without even telling the other. The wisdom of such a procedure was graphically illustrated a dozen times over. The alien's work, when he did it, was thorough. The operative in Pittsburgh had tried to fight back the alien's telepathic overtures, as instructed, and suffered a burst of wrath that had left him blubbering in a corner for three days until a crew of Hoffman Center physicians located him and straightened him out with stimulants and glucose. More and more, the alien's puzzlement and frustration and anger began to seep through in the contact reports, and Paul and Jean watched and nodded approvingly.

Meanwhile, other steps were taken. Three times, when they were certain the alien had left a locality, they ordered cleanup squads to raid his former quarters, quizzing neighbors, asking multitudes of idiotic questions, uncovering half a dozen descriptions and leads—all of which they assiduously ignored. They began stabbing erratically at locations where the alien had *not* yet been, raids carried out with a relentlessness and singleness of mind that left the unfortunates who were questioned shaking in their boots. Even the agents themselves were confused as to the purpose of these raids, and were cheerfully allowed to remain confused. Still other tactics were pursued, a series of disjointed, uncoordinated, abortive and harassing procedures, as though the whole search had suddenly fallen into the hands of a madman. A rocket ship bound for Venus was delayed four days beyond an opposition, adding a half-million dollars to the cost of fueling it. A whole series of road blocks was thrown up between New York and New Philadelphia, virtually paralyzing commercial traffic between the cities for two days, for no coherent reason. An order went out, quite arbitrarily, to apprehend and search all passengers on the great St. Louis-New York rolling-roads route, and Robert Roberts put in a gruelling week trying to soothe the ruffled feelings of businessmen who had been held up in transit, and companies whose products had spoiled when the swift-moving strips had been halted for the shakedown.

Rumors began to drift out, rumors that there *was* an alien from the stars at large, that Federal Security was waging a vast underground battle to capture him before the news broke out. Telecasts buzzed with "it was alleged" and "unconfirmed reports say." The tension mounted daily. Bit by bit, carefully sifted crumbs of information were dropped into the minds of the Psi-Highs who were still in the alien's path, and all around the alien's path. Long hours were spent in the headquarters suite, planning and coordinating the pattern. But in the end, it was a pattern well chosen and worth the effort, for it was soon evident that the alien was heading for the great eastern metropolitan area which surrounded the capital city as though he were drawn to the lodestone rock.

No attempt was made to contact *him;* quite the contrary. All the alien's overtures yielded him no response other than futile attempts at shielding; no analysis of any contact was even attempted, and this knowledge was planted so that the alien was sure to learn it. Warnings of traps were planted in his path, "secret" knowledge of closing dragnets and carefully devised Psi-High weapons to be used against him. Occasionally such warnings were followed by abortive raids, always either too early to meet him or too late, always carried out by psi-negative Security men who had no more idea what they were doing than the man in the moon. But one by one, key facts were planted, pointing always in one direction, and always the alien moved toward the headquarters area.

Paul Faircloth and Jean Sanders seldom left the hotel even for a few minutes. Their job was to keep the pattern moving, and to plot out their individual tactics quite apart from each other. It was wearing; as the tension mounted, both of them grew more haggard. Paul had not found time to shave in a week, and there were dark circles under the girl's eyes. Much of the time she just sat, tense, listening, waiting; other times she helped him work as he fed data into the field computer squatting in the suite. But even in the tension and exhaustion of the work, neither of them could forget the simple, awful fact that Paul Faircloth had been identified as a Psi High, and that somehow, they would have to rearrange all the plans they had had for the future.

Each morning they spread the reports out on the table before them. "Closer," Paul said one day. "And it's on his own volition. He hasn't been pushed. In fact, he'd been left out in the cold and he doesn't seem to like it."

The girl nodded, and glanced at the papers. "He's definitely trying to ask questions, now, when he contacts. Karns' call last night showed that better than any other. And of course Karns didn't know any answers."

Faircloth nodded. "None of them know the answers. That's the beauty of it. Try as he will, he doesn't get anywhere."

"Not yet." The girl rose, walking across the room. "Paul, I'm afraid. We're shooting in the dark. We don't know what we're fighting against."

"Are you sorry you're in on it?"

"Oh, no!" She turned around, her face stricken. "It's not that. It's just—" His mind was suddenly filled with shadows, impressions struggling to get through, impressions that would make the use of words ridiculous. "Oh, Paul, I'm afraid for *you,* for both of us. If anything should happen—"

"Nothing's going to happen."

"But what about *us?* If something goes wrong—Roberts knows about you—"

"I'd rather Roberts knew than Ben Towne."

The girl's eyes were wide with fright. She seemed so small and helpless. "But we shouldn't be together! Oh, Paul, why did Roberts have to find out? Why did *anyone* have to find out?" And then she was sobbing in his arms, and he held her close, trying to comfort her.

"Jeannie," he murmured. "This just doesn't do any good."

"But it's so unfair! Why shouldn't I be allowed to marry you if I want to?"

"You know why as well as I do. Because *people are afraid of us.* There's nothing we can do about it, that's just the way people are. They're *always* afraid of people who seem to threaten the way things have always been. So they passed the laws, and they think they're right."

"*Ben Towne* thinks they're right!" she burst out scornfully. Her tears were hot on his cheek.

"Towne pushed the laws through, but he couldn't have done it alone. People are afraid of someone carrying a single psi-positive gene, like you and me. What would they do if the gene were doubled? How could *we* tell what our children would be like? Look, Jeannie, *think!* You're just now learning how to use your psi-powers, and look what you're doing! You can almost get through to me, and I've had no formal training at all. I've been underground, just training myself as best I could. You've almost reached your limit. Dr. Abrams says you'll have almost complete control in five years, and I could too, with the proper training. What would our children be like, with the psi-factor on both sides?"

"Well, what would be wrong with it?" The girl was fighting back the tears. "Are we such monsters? Have we done anything so terrible that we have to be caged like animals and kept under control like criminals?"

Paul shook his head. "People fear anything different, and they only know what they've been told. Ben Towne has been a vicious enemy, and enough people believe him to give him tremendous power. And there's not one thing we can do about it." He pulled a handkerchief from his pocket and dabbed at her face with it. "It doesn't even pay to think about it, right now. We've got a job to do, Jeannie. It might be the most important thing that Psi-Highs have ever tried to do. We can't flop on this job."

"But Towne will just turn it against us."

"Not if we work it right, he won't. And I've got a hunch that we're working it right."

10

WHEN IT SEEMED that the strike-point could only be hours away, the visiphone buzzed and Roberts' worried face appeared on the screen.

"Paul," he said sharply, "there are some bad rumors around. I think we're in trouble."

Paul cursed. "What kind of rumors?"

"All kinds," said Roberts sourly. "They're saying the hunt for the alien is a fraud, that nobody is doing anything at all about it. There were a couple of out-and-out charges that Psi-Highs are teaming up with the alien to make an attempt on the government."

"Moons of Mars, can't *somebody* put the lid on that man?"

"That wasn't even Towne's work. It was some Isolationist senator on one of their propaganda shows. There's talk that the Liberals are purposely blocking an investigation of the Hoffman Center and their Psi-High program, and the President is out on a limb now that might break off any minute. I think Ben Towne is planning a direct confrontation, and that means we're running out of time. You know that Congress hasn't been joined into two solid political parties for over two hundred years, but it's beginning to happen now, and it could be a bloody battle. If Towne can get the Civil Rights Party to swing their votes away from the President, it could force a general election."

"Who's the leader of the Civil Rights men?" Faircloth's voice was sharp.

"That's just the thing. It has been Mike Veriday. His son is a Psi-High, but his political stock has taken an awful nose-dive since this rumor campaign started. The polls have got him trailing Kingsley from Kentucky by thirteen percent and losing ground fast. Now Kingsley, it seems, is in some unpleasant financial trouble, and some of Towne's old cronies in the Senate have offered to clear him of some nasty charges if he plays along." He paused for a long moment. "We haven't got much time, Paul."

"Well, I hope we don't need much. But I think you can call in as many of our men as you need to. If things get too hot, list Jean and me as fugitives and throw out a dragnet for us. Because I think we'll be working very much outside the law in another day or so."

Roberts blinked at him. "Better tell me what you're planning, Paul."

"I think the less you know about it the better. Just one thing, though. You remember Eagle Rock? The place we built up in the Adirondacks that summer when we were in college? Put three men at a number where I can reach them, and give them the location of Eagle Rock. Then tell them to stand by with a fast jet scooter. Got that? And don't let *this* leak, no matter what happens."

"I wish you'd tell me—"

"We're fighting for our lives now, Bob. And for every Psi-High in the country. I can't tell you a thing more."

Roberts nodded, then shrugged helplessly. "Eagle Rock," he said. "You can count on it."

Paul flipped the set off and winked at Jean. Together they settled back to wait for the alien to make his last contact.

11

HE STRUCK at ten o'clock that evening, with a ferocity beyond their worst expectations.

They had known that he was near. The reports had come in, and they had plotted and calculated his pathway, and waited. It was only a matter of time. The carefully planted information built a tangled, devious circle with a single Psi-High individual in the center.

Jean Sanders.

It had to be Jean. Paul hated it, he wished it could be he, that somehow he could take the blow and shield her, but Jean Sanders was the only possible person to bait the trap. Her psi-powers had been developed carefully and painstakingly for years under the care of Dr. Reuben Abrams and his staff at the Hoffman Medical Center. A Psi-High individual was helpless to use his powers without training; just as a child was trained through long, grueling years to use his ordinary mental faculties of thought and perception and logic, a psi-positive mind required training to control its powers of extrasensory perception and psychokinetic control, if its powers were ever to be used.

Paul knew that all too well. He too was Psi-High, but he had not even known it for years. He had not realized, in his teens, when he had plagued and baited the two Psi-High boys in his high school class, that there might be a time factor in psi-positive development. Other Psi-Highs showed the signs of abnormal sensory apparatus at the age of one, or three, or seven; invariably the schools spotted them, tested them, registered them, and sent them out into a life of fear and suspicion and hatred. They were considered freaks, the more dangerous because there was no physical identification that could be used to separate them from ordinary human beings. And certain men had recognized the power waiting for the man who took advantage of the people's fears. Ambition is blinding; certain men could see the potential danger, real or imaginary, that might arise if Psi-High minds were to work their way into the government, into law or the judiciary. But Psi-High minds matured at different ages, and at different times. And some, like Paul Faircloth, slipped through the barrage of testing undetected, only to discover later that it really wasn't the backs of the cards they were reading at all, but the minds of their opponents that were holding the cards.

The faculty was feeble, in people like Paul. He could not

read minds. He could not sort and integrate the confused ten-
drils of conscious and unconscious thought that broke like an
endless stream from a human mind; he could not separate the
reality of here-and-now thinking from the strands of fantasy
and memory and supposition and frustration and desire and
half-understanding and confusion that lay beneath the surface
of those minds. He could detect falsehood and he could feel
suspicion; he could sense love as he had never felt it before,
and he could feel himself gripped in the helpless frustration
of pity; he could savor excitement with a thousand tingling
nerves, and he could sense the blackest depths of despair, but
he could not sort them out into a coherent picture of the
thoughts streaming from a human mind. It took a long hard
training for a Psi-High mind to do that, and no shortcut had
ever been found. Paul Faircloth could not do these things, and
he knew he could not.

But Jean Sanders could. That was why she was waiting in
the room with him when the alien struck.

She was walking across the room when it happened. She
stopped suddenly, with a gasp. Even Paul caught the wave of
fear and revulsion that swept from her mind. She stared for
a moment, terrified, and then sank to the floor, gripping her
head with her hands. Paul watched helplessly as she tried to
fight back the powerful invasion, in spite of herself. "Please,"
she gasped, white-faced. "Get me a pillow. Then—then listen—"

"Don't fight him," Paul whispered. "Let him in. Let him
clear in. And then—jump on him. For all you're worth, *dig,
dig deep.*"

Her eyes became huge, like the eyes of an animal, frightened beyond hope, cornered, attacked and helpless to fight
back. Her neck strained back, and her teeth clenched. The
blood drained from her face as she began moaning. "I can't,
Paul—" she cried, "I—I can't get in—"

"You've got to—" Frantically, Paul tried to thrust out with his mind, tried to dig through the mind-staggering wall of power he felt in the room. The alien was close, very close, and the presence of his mind was almost overwhelming. Paul tried to break through. . . . Suddenly, he felt a pang of white heat sear through his brain, driving him back, a sharp, savage stroke that doubled him up, clasping his hands helplessly to his ears. Suddenly it was gone, as swiftly as it had come. He stood panting for a moment. Then he managed to stumble over to Jean. She was not responding; he listened, heard the slow pounding of her heart. He shook her, gently; her eyes flickered open, her face filled with horror and loathing. "Oh, Paul, I got—I got so little—"

"What did you get?"

"Nothing—a picture or two, nothing more. Oh, he was so *strong*, I couldn't make a dent—"

"What pictures?"

She sat up, panting. "Nothing—definite. Ben Towne—yes, there was something about him—just the flash of a mental picture, no rationale connected with it. And some papers, some sort of file—" She clasped her hands to her head. "He—he stripped me clean! I can't—"

"Jeannie! *There must have been something else.*"

She looked up at him, a strange light in her eyes. "I don't understand it," she whispered. "He seemed to be trying to *tell* me something. There was a picture of a farm—yes, a farm. And a dog— And blood on a pair of pants—"

Paul sat back, staring at her stupidly. All at once, something flashed in his mind, an idea so incredible that he hardly dared to think of it. An instant later he was on his feet, staring at the girl. "He was trying to *tell* you this?"

"Yes. *Something.*"

"And no mistaking the picture?"

"Never. It was clear as crystal."

He began throwing clothes into a bag as the girl sat there, watching him in growing alarm. "Stay here," he said. "I'll call you."

"Paul—where—"

"It's my show, now, Jeannie. You wait here, you'll be all right. Rest, and say a prayer or two. Because I think I've got this alien pinned down for sure, this time."

12

IT WAS AN incredibly dangerous move, but it was utterly necessary. Paul found a visiphone booth in the rear of a station with no people around, and quickly threw an adapter across the lens of the pickup and spun a roll of tape into it. The tape started when the party at the other end flipped on the switch, and the conversation was brief. Paul gave the address of a roof garden apartment in Central Washington, and then disconnected. After removing the film, he dialed a number he had given Roberts a few hours before. Ted Marino's face appeared, and Paul heaved a sigh of relief. "Sorry, Ted, but I'm afraid you're back in the game. How many men do you have?"

"Two."

"Both Psi-High?"

"Certainly."

Paul nodded. "All right, we're beyond the law from now on. If you or the others want out, take off."

Marino's dark eyes sparked. "Roberts said this was the kill."

"It's not the kill you think. But it's a kill, all right. Take the men to this address." He gave the roof garden number. "Have a jet scooter there, and see that nobody spots it. Use Federal Security insignia. Sound off loud and clear if anything goes wrong. I'll meet you there."

He rang off, and soon was rising high above the city in his own jet scooter. In ten minutes he had reached the roof garden, and set the little ship gently down. He walked inside, and sat down in the darkness, and waited.

Moments later another jet scooter landed. Marino walked in with two men whom Paul remembered vaguely. He nodded to them, and they also sat down. Paul fingered the shocker in his pocket, his nerves screaming a thousand warnings in his ears.

The guard robot on the ground floor bleeped sharply. Paul reached for the lock release switch, and heard the elevator start to whine. He unlocked the door and left it ajar, then motioned to one of the men. "Cover the hallway, and back them up when they come. Don't be worried about who it is."

The man disappeared down the hall. Paul sat quietly; he heard the elevator open. There were footsteps, and tapping sound. The footsteps stopped at the door.

"Come on in," Paul called out. "Bob'll be here in just a minute."

The door swung open, and Secretary Benjamin Towne walked into the room, followed by two tight-faced men. One of the men had a hand in his jacket pocket. Towne blinked at Faircloth, and his grin began to fade into alarm. "Who in hell are you?"

"One of Roberts' men."

"Roberts said you had the alien here," Towne snarled. His green eyes peered around the room.

Marino swung on the man to the right, bringing him down with one short blow. Paul slapped Towne's cane to the floor, and pounced on the other guard like a cat. The secretary staggered against the door jamb, cursing a steady stream. Moments later the bodyguards were helpless, and Paul and Marino were dragging Towne out to the middle of the room.

"The files," Paul said sharply. "Where do you keep them?"

"What files?"

"The private files you've been keeping, Mr. Secretary. The blackmail files, the personal dossiers you've compiled on every registered Psi-High in existence. Your backstop, Mr. Secretary—the files you planned to use to personally break every Psi-High on the wheel if for some reason you couldn't beat them down legally. All right, I want those files. Now."

Towne's eyes were deadly; his breath came heavily. "You freaks will never get away with this."

"The files, Mr. Secretary."

Towne's eyes went around the room fearfully. "The boys know where they are," he said finally, his voice so low it was hardly audible.

"Any duplicates?"

"Not of the files you want."

Paul nodded to Towne's men. "Take these thugs down and revive them," he told Marino. "And get the files. Then turn the boys over to Roberts. Tell him that they're to be held in maximum security until this is over." He turned back to Ben Towne. "As for you, you're taking a little ride."

"When this hits the papers, it'll be the end of the road for you freaks," Towne snarled. "You can't stop it now."

"We'll see," said Faircloth. "Now shut up and get moving."

They left the cane in the room. Paul helped Marino load the man aboard the jet scooter. "Take him up to Eagle Rock. Keep him there. Dismantle the engine, if you have to, but keep him there. I'll join you in a few hours."

Marino nodded. "Should I report to Roberts?"

"Don't bother. Roberts would have a stroke. I trapped Towne into coming over here by using a dummy visiphone tape of Roberts, which will put him in enough hot water as it is."

"And where are you going?"

"West, for a few hours. I've got a visit to make. I've got to see a man about a dog."

13 THE FARMER blinked across the table at him, red-eyed and suspicious. "I don't know what you want," he was saying, querulously. "I didn't ask for no trouble with your Federal men. They asked me all them questions, and I told them—"

"That's all right," said Faircloth. "I'm just rechecking. You were the first human being the alien contacted, as far as we can tell. The ship landed on your property, didn't it?"

The farmer nodded. "Over by the river. Scrub oak and elms standing over there, on the bluff. Haven't never cleared it because it'd be too rocky to farm."

"All right, all right," said Faircloth sharply. "I want you to tell me what happened that night."

The farmer's eyes flitted to Faircloth's face, and back down to the table. "I already told you twenty times," he whined. "Why pick on me? I couldn't help it he happened to stop here. Heard him on the porch about ten o'clock at night. I was just gettin' ready for bed. And he said he was travelin' through and wanted something to eat. We don't see strangers around here very often, mister—" he looked up at Faircloth fearfully. "I— I looked at him, and he seemed all right to me. My eyes was tired, like I said, I couldn't see him too well, but he come in, and ate. Didn't want to bed him down, but he said he had to make on for Des Moines anyway."

Faircloth watched the man's eyes. "Details, Mr. Bettendorf. You've skipped a few things, haven't you? I have your original statement here, filed by our field agent." He pulled out a sheaf of papers and scanned them in the dim kitchen light. "Says something about your dog barking—"

The farmer' face went white. "Anything wrong with that? I reckon the dog *did* bark. I don't remember."

"And you went to open the door, and the stranger was there on the porch, eh?"

The farmer nodded his head eagerly. "I told you everything."

"And you brought him in, and fed him, and then sent him on his way?"

"That's right, just like I said."

"You're a liar," said Faircloth. He eyed the man coldly. "Try the story over again."

The farmer jolted to his feet, his eyes feverish. "I done just like I said, you can't call me no liar! I heard the dog barking—"

"And you opened the door, and saw the stranger there." Faircloth's voice was sharp. "So then what? Step by step. Minute by minute. I mean it, mister, *I want the truth.*"

"I—I looked at him—"

"With just the porch light on?"

"That's right, just like I just showed you—"

"And what did the stranger say?"

"He said, 'I'm a traveler, and I'd like something to eat.'"

"And what did his voice sound like?"

The farmer faltered. "It was funny—like gravel in a tin can. A funny kind of a voice—"

"And where was the dog all this time?"

The farmer blanched. "He—he was somewhere outside. He saw it was all right—"

"Where's the dog now?"

"I sold him. I mean he ran away. You can't keep a dog forever, mister."

Faircloth's face was very close to the old man's. "The stranger was out on the porch, and you talked to him, and let him come in. And then what happened?"

"I—he sat down at the table, I think—I—I—"

"You went over to get some food from the stove, didn't you?"

"Yes, yes, that's right—"

"And then you saw blood on his pants, didn't you? And you remembered hearing your dog give a yelp, out there in the yard, didn't you? And that stranger had blood all over his pants and boots, didn't he?"

The farmer's eyes were wide with fear, and he was shaking his head helplessly. "No—no—"

"And so *you took that shotgun off the rack over there and you shot him, didn't you?*"

And then the old man's face was in his hands, and he was bending over the table, crying like a baby—huge, fearful sobs racking his bony shoulders. "He killed my dog," he choked out. "He killed my Brownie, gave him a kick that split his head wide open. He didn't have to do that to poor old Brownie, did he? I knew he was a bad one when he did that. Yes, I shot him, right through the chest. Buried him down by the river, what was left of him."

14

THE NEWS broke to the nation that night, and the country went into a panic unequalled since the days of the Chinese Confrontation. Paul Faircloth spent an hour on the visiphone from Des Moines, talking to Robert Roberts, going over the whole business, from beginning to end, while the Security chief stared at him as though he were demented. Finally Roberts put a call through to the President. Half an hour later, while Faircloth was making his way back to Washington, Roberts was in top-secret conference with the Senate leaders and the Cabinet and finally with the President himself. At last the carefully prepared news broke. It was an official White House news conference, and it was barely over when the radios and TVs were carrying the announcement.

Faircloth brought his plane down in Washington. He saw the crowd swarming across the landing strip before he could get unstrapped. A dozen flashbulbs popped, and between him and the Security limousine was a tight circle of reporters.

"How long has the alien been at large, Mr. Faircloth?" one of them asked.

"Sorry. The chief will have to answer that."

"Is there any doubt that he's telepathic?"

"No doubt whatsoever. I know that from personal experience. It's the only way he could move freely in the population."

"How was he first detected?"

Paul smiled to himself. "The President told you that, didn't he? A Psi-High citizen spotted him in Des Moines. The Psi-Highs have been on his trail ever since."

One of the reporters was tugging at his arm. "There's been a lot of rumor about some kind of—well, conspiracy between the alien invader and the Psi-Highs in this country."

Paul frowned. "If that were true, would we be working twenty-four hours a day to trap him? Use your head, man. I know the rumors, but I can speak for the Psi-Highs, and I think Commissioner Roberts will back me up on this: the alien is menacing our very civilization. He's struck out against one of our most beloved public servants, Secretary Ben Towne, in an attempt to undermine our government and prepare our planet for a full-scale invasion. There isn't a Psi-High citizen in the country who will rest until the monster is caught, and until Secretary Towne has been returned safely to Washington."

"But what about Towne's anti-Psi legislation? He's always hated Psi-Highs."

"Nonsense. Towne has been a loyal servant of the North American people. He's fought for what he thought was right, and has exposed himself to great dangers and personal vilification in order to do it. Sometimes he hasn't seen the Psi-Highs' side of things, but that's not a matter for us to be vindicative about at a time like this." He looked around the circle soberly. "The fact remains that he's in the hands of a dangerous enemy, and it's our job to save him if it can possibly be done." He nodded, and stepped into the Security limousine. It honked its way through the crowd, then dipped down into the government tunnel that lead to Central Washington and Capitol Hill.

Inside the car, Paul picked up a newspaper and peered at it eagerly. The full-color picture of the President's grave face stared out at him in 3-D, with photos of Robert Roberts and Ben Towne on either side. It was an old picture of Towne, almost a flattering picture. Paul grinned as he read the story rapidly:

SECRETARY TOWNE KIDNAPED FROM SECRET MEETING
PRESIDENT REVEALS ALIEN TELEPATH AT LARGE

"The President of the North American States revealed tonight in a special press conference that Medical Affairs Secretary Benjamin Towne was kidnaped from a secret meeting with Federal Security agents last night in what was described as the first step in a plan for large-scale invasion of Earth by an alien race from another planet. The President reported that one alien, believed to be fully telepathic, has been at large in the country since his landing near Gutenberg, Iowa, last May 26th.

"The alien's presence was first detected by a loyal Psi-High citizen of Des Moines, Iowa, and was reported immediately to the Federal Security Commission. Robert H. Roberts, Chief of Security, has been active in directing a nationwide dragnet to capture the alien.

"Secretary Towne left his home last night at 11:00 P.M. in response to a call allegedly from Commissioner Roberts. It is believed that the call was forged by the use of a dummy-film; the secretary was reported missing when he did not return home. The two aides who accompanied him apparently suffered severely from the encounter with the alien's telepathic powers; their condition is reported satisfactory but they were unavailable for questioning at the Hoffman Medical Center this morning.

"The President commented on the excellent and selfless work of certain Psi-High citizens during the past months in the course of a manhunt that has been shrouded in secrecy. The alien's telepathic powers invariably overcame the efforts of psi-negative individuals, but through the efforts of the Psi-Highs, Commissioner Roberts has expressed every hope of ending the search within days and securing Secretary Towne's release. It is believed that Towne was kidnaped by the alien in order to obtain information regarding the extent of psi-development in our culture, prior to a large-scale invasion.

"Notable among the directors of the nationwide search is Security Agent Paul L. Faircloth of this city, whose work with Security has been so secret that the fact of his Psi-High status has been carefully concealed, even from Federal Registry—"

Faircloth flipped the page, glancing at the smaller headlines. An interview with Dr. Abrams reporting the training program for Psi-Highs in progress at the Hoffman Center; a long article, discussing the value of Psi-High powers in combatting a ruthless telepathic alien force; an article by Roberts, very carefully worded, explaining that if one telepathic alien had come to Earth, others could be expected to follow. Roberts expressed the opinion that human psi-positives were the nation's strongest safeguard against such an invasion. "The time has come," the article quoted Roberts, "for the people of the North American States to recognize that in such an emergency as this, fire must be fought with fire. The powers of the alien now are too great for even the best-trained Psi-High to oppose completely. But with further training and proper development of the psi-positive resources in the population, there should be little chance for an invasion which depends on the telepathic power of the aliens to succeed in the future."

Faircloth carefully folded the paper and spoke to the driver of the limousine. The car emerged from the next tunnel exit and sped north. Paul waited, impatiently. At last he stepped out of the car at the secret Baltimore headquarters. Moments later he was holding Jean Sanders in his arms, while Robert Roberts, across the room, looked slightly embarrassed but enormously pleased with himself.

15

"IT WAS HANDLED beautifully," Faircloth was saying. "The timing was perfect, and there's no question that it will go across." He looked at Jean. "You're sure you got everything through to him when he contacted you the second time?"

She nodded. Her face was still pale. "He turned me inside out. Cleaned out everything I knew. I didn't resist. And then, when we'd heard from you, he contacted me a third time, and I knew that we were right. He's been in touch with me ever since. He'll be here soon."

Faircloth nodded to Roberts. "And you've arranged for the fake raids to start up through New England?"

Roberts nodded. "Everything's under control. Marino has a mockup spaceship ready for takeoff, and we've been moving artillery into the area near Eagle Rock to blast it down. Fortunately, there aren't too many nosey people up around there." He grinned. "The pictures will probably come out pretty bad, but after all—field conditions, you know—what can people expect? It will certainly *look* like the same sort of ship that landed out in Iowa, and there won't be enough left when the blasting is finished to tell for sure whether the mangled mess that they drag out of it later is man, alien, or oily rags. Those guns do a good job."

Something touched Faircloth's mind, lightly, like a timid knock. He swung around, his eyes wide. "He's here," he said, and saw that Jean already knew. "Down below. Tell him to come up."

She nodded, and closed her eyes. Moments later they heard footsteps on the stairs, hesitant footsteps. The door swung open. They stared at him for a moment, and then both Paul and Roberts were wringing his hand, offering him a glass. He nodded, murmuring his thanks, and sank down on the cot they had ready for him.

"You must be exhausted," Paul said quietly.

"I am, I am," he said. "Mind if I lie down?"

He was an ordinary looking man, slender, about thirty, and very pale. A little disappointing, Paul thought. Of course, a single-factor Psi-High had no distinguishing physical characteristics so there was really no reason to expect a double-factor psi-positive to look any different. But somehow Paul had half expected a godlike creature. Instead here was just a wary, frightened looking, tired young man. His face was mild, with a trace of sadness about it. But his eyes were clear and sharp, and his mouth was a grim line, as he sank back on the couch. "I was afraid you were never going to spot it," he said. "For a while it looked as if the whole thing was backfiring on me. I mean, when Towne started publishing the scare stories and it began to look as if he might actually succeed in forcing an election. That really scared me, and right about then you started your cat-and-mouse game."

Faircloth nodded. "We had no choice. We didn't know, of course, that the alien had been destroyed before he even got started. And you didn't dare to reveal to anyone just what you were or what you were trying to do."

The man shook his head. "There wasn't a soul I was sure I could trust, not even Psi-Highs, until I contacted Jean, and then saw from the President's announcement that you were on to me but weren't saying anything. But it turned out better this way, much better. Originally I'd planned to kill Towne and then let you capture me, counting on you to handle the cover stories the right way. Then nobody but you people would ever have known that the alien was killed less than two hours after he had landed."

Faircloth smiled. "The computer even listed that as one possibility. Low probability, but that was on the basis of what we knew. We hadn't even considered it. Yet every living Psi-High has known, for a long time, that someday two Psi-Highs would have a child, laws or no laws. We could only guess what the child might be like."

The man looked at them sadly. "The child would be lonely beyond words," he said. "He would be able to hide, yes. He would be able to tone down his psi-powers in order to appear like an ordinary Psi-High, roughly comparable, in a psi-negative, to voluntarily having both eyes and ears destroyed. But whatever happened, a double-Psi could never reveal the truth about himself. Not even to his closest friends."

"And you knew from the start that the real alien had been killed?"

"Almost as soon as it happened. He died in agony. He had a powerful mind; ordinary Psi-Highs must only have picked up a ripple, but a hundred miles away in Des Moines I got a shower that nearly killed me. I knew that was from nothing human, not even another double-Psi. So I went down to the place and picked the details out of the farmer's brain, masquerading as a Security agent. He was too frightened to tell anybody what he had done, and of course nobody later paid too much attention to him anyway." The man shifted wearily on the cot. "The alien must have been working so hard trying to maintain his disguise that he missed what the farmer was thinking until it was too late. But as soon as I knew that an alien with that kind of power had landed, I knew what I had to do: step into his shoes, pretend that I was he, and somehow give human Psi-Highs a chance to prove to the whole world that they were loyal, reliable human beings and not some new kind of dangerous freaks."

16

"OF COURSE Towne will fight," said Roberts later, when the man had drifted off into an exhausted sleep. "He's clever, and resourceful. When we 'rescue' him from Eagle Rock, he's going to know exactly what happened."

Jean Sanders laughed happily. "And everyone is going to believe Dr. Abrams' considered opinion that his mind has been affected by his terrible experience with the alien. Which is going to leave him helpless." She looked at Paul. "And that's something I'm vindictive enough to want to see. I want to see Ben Towne helpless, for once."

Paul grinned. "You will. Things will have moved 'way ahead of him, by then. And of course, there will be a physical and mental examination. It will be a pity that the alien left his mind in such a state of shock and delusion, but maybe, after a few months of psychiatric treatment, someone will find out the *real* reason why he hates Psi-Highs so much. Of course, we can guess: an imperfect man, with that clubfoot of his, fighting to prove that he really *is not* a cripple in a world of normal men, fighting and hating the ones who are not physically flawed . . . and hating even more viciously those few of us he regards as super-perfect. And probably not even realizing that that's why he hates us. If he could only be helped to see it and make peace with it and with us, we'll have a powerful fighter on our side instead of against us." He looked around at the others, his face grave. "We can't afford to have the world against us again, not ever. *That* part of the news broadcast was perfectly true: there *was* an alien. He *was* telepathic. And there will be others coming, maybe in a year, maybe in five, or ten, or a hundred." He leaned back wearily in the relaxer. "What happened this time, turned out to be an incredibly lucky break for us, thanks to our double-Psi friend here. But *we* must never forget the things about this alien scare that were true."

Jean smiled, and put her arm around him. "Others will come, sometime, yes. But in the meantime, hundreds of Psi-Highs are going to be in intensive training. Psi-Highs are going to be marrying Psi-Highs. When other aliens come, they'll find the Earth well guarded." Her eyes drifted to the sleeping man on the cot, and then returned to Paul's and held them. "And when they do come, there'll be others—like *him*—to stop them."

PART THREE

Mirror, Mirror

Somewhere down on the surface of Saturn the Enemy was waiting.

The Earth outpost on the Satellite ship orbiting Saturn knew that he was there, with his four great ships and the unimaginable power that had brought him from whatever place he had come. But the Earth outpost did not know why he had come, and now they did not know what he intended to do.

He had come into the solar system, and struck with pointless savagery, and then fled to a place where Earth ships could not follow him. Now he waited there, silent and enigmatic. His very presence was intolerable: the Earth outpost knew they had to fight him, somehow, but the fight was on his terms, on the battleground he had chosen.

It was an impossible war from the very start, a vicious war, draining the last reserves of the tiny group of Earthmen who had to fight it. It engulfed their waking hours and tortured their

sleep with nightmares. There was no time to stop and ask
themselves: why are we fighting this war?

They were fighting it, that was enough. Only the Enemy
knew why. . . .

1

THE WAITING was the most terrible
part of all for John Provost.

There was no chronometer in the day room of the Satellite
ship, but Provost had his own private chronometer buried in
his skull, somewhere in that vague impersonal space that lay
between his left ear and his left eyebrow, deep down, ticking
away hours, minutes, seconds, ridiculous fractions of ridiculous
segments of seconds, marking them off against him inexorably,
the epitome of all timepieces. It was there in his head and he
couldn't get away from it, not even when his shift was over
and he was back in Relief, laboriously rebuilding the fragments
of John Provost that the Enemy had torn away. Now, almost
whole and fresh again, he could hear the chronometer clicking
away against him, and once more he was certain that it was
the *waiting* he feared far more than he feared the Enemy.

Almost time, Provost. Almost your turn to go down
again. . . .

He paced the day room of the Satellite ship and felt sweat
trickle down his chest from the waiting and the silence. Always,
in the last hour before his shift, he lived in an envelope of self-
induced silence. Canned music blared from the wall speaker,
unnaturally loud, but Provost did not hear it. There was talking and chatter in the day room, harsh laughter all about him,

noises of glasses clinking, feet shuffling. A dozen men were here, but to Provost the day room was like a TV with the sound turned off. He was utterly isolated, and that was the way he wanted it.

He rubbed wet palms against his trousers and waited.

Nobody looked at him, of course. The men knew that his shift was next. Nobody spoke to him; he might smile and answer them pleasantly, or he might turn on them, savagely and without warning, like a cornered rat. It had happened before, with others. He was like a crossbow with the spring drawn tight, waiting to be triggered, and nobody wanted to tamper with him twenty minutes before shift change. Everyone knew he wouldn't be responsible for what he might do.

And with every passing second the spring was pulled tighter. That was what made the waiting so terrible.

He went below and stepped into a hot foam shower, felt the powerful muscles of his shoulders and neck relax a trifle. Briefly he thought of the Turner girl. Would she be in Relief when he returned? Of course, there were others equally well trained to help the men through the period of childish regression that inevitably occurred when their shifts were over and the pressure suddenly off—the only way they could rebuild their mental resources for another shift—but to John Provost, the Turner girl seemed better than any of the others. They'd actually begun to be good friends as he had come, slowly, to trust her under circumstances in which trust was difficult if not impossible. And then that new woman that DepPsych had sent out from the Hoffman Center, Dorie Kendall—what about her? Help, or hindrance? Dangerous, sending out new people at a time like this. Yet, she'd *listened* when he'd told her how he could use his Analogue to take his mind and sensorium down to Saturn's surface without actually leaving the Satellite ship at all. Maybe she'd do. Maybe she might even be able to help him, somehow.

Provost dressed quickly now as the fear grew stronger in his mind. There was no use trying to fight it down; he knew that from long experience. It was far more exhausting to try than just to give in to it, start counting the minutes to Relief from *now* instead of when the shift began. It made things balance better in his mind that way, even if it made the DepPsych people scream and wring their hands. Well, let them scream. There was nothing they knew about this Idiot War that he didn't know—absolutely nothing. He was an expert on this war. They couldn't even imagine what an expert he was.

He checked at the Control board. "Provost on."

"Are you steady?" the voice from Control asked.

Provost grunted.

"All right, here's the report." The voice hesitated an instant. "I don't think you're going to like it very much."

"Let's have it."

"Dead quiet on the front all through the last shift," Control said.

Provost blinked. "Quiet!"

"That's the report."

Provost shivered. "What do you suppose they're cooking up *now?*"

"I wish I could tell you." The voice from Control was puzzled and sympathetic. "They're brewing *something* down there, that's certain. Chances are it'll be nasty, too. They haven't given us a quiet shift in months." Provost could almost see the face of the controller, somewhere deep in the lower regions of the Satellite ship. "You may be the one to get hit with it, John, whatever it is. But then, maybe it'll stay quiet for you, too."

"Not with my luck," said Provost. "Well, I'm going in now."

He stepped into the Analogue cubicle with the green flasher over the door, found the cockpit in the darkness, fit his damp hands into the grips. He shook the Analogue helmet down on his head until it was comfortable. He didn't try to tell himself that *he* wasn't really going down to Saturn's surface, that only a tiny bit of metal and stamped circuitry was going down under his mental control. DepPsych had given up on *that* line of comfort long ago. Provost knew all too well that he didn't have to be on the surface in the flesh in order for the Enemy to rip him apart. He closed his eyes in the darkness, trying to relax.

Still waiting, now, for the signal to move in. He didn't know which man he was relieving. DepPsych said it was better not to know. Even the signals from the Analogues were monitored so he wouldn't have a hint. Every man operated his Analogue differently—but could the Enemy tell the difference?

Provost was certain that they could. Not that it seemed to make any difference, to them.

"Countdown." He heard the buzzer sound, and he crushed down with all his power on the hand grips. He felt the jolting thud as he slammed into full Analogue contact, and something deep in his mind began screaming *now! now! now!*

He dropped away into nothing.

Moments later he knew that he was on the surface, even though a corner of his mind was aware of the sticky hand grips, the dark closeness of the Analogue cubicle. Before him he could see the great yawning chasms of ice on Saturn's surface stretching out into the distance. Yellow-grey light reflected down from the Rings. He could sense the devastating pressure of gravity here even though he could not feel it. Overhead, a roiling sea of methane and ammonia clouds, crashing lightning, the unspeakable violence of Saturn's continual war with itself.

And somewhere beyond the place where he was, the Enemy.

There was no contact, at first. Provost groped, and found nothing. He could always tell their presence, just as he was certain now that they could tell his. But that was as far as he could go. *They* planned. *They* moved. If *they* were ready, they struck. If they weren't ready, they didn't.

And until they struck, he was helpless. There was nothing for him to fight against. All he could do was wait. For what? He did not know. But always before, there had been *something*.

Now, nothing. Not a whisper. He waited, sick with fear. He knew how brutal the Enemy could be. He knew the viciousness of their blows, the savagery, the cunning. These were things he could fight, turning their own weapons against them. But *nothingness* was something else.

How could he fight nothing? He couldn't. He could only wait.

He stretched his mind, groping for them. Then, suddenly, he felt a gentle brush of contact . . . they were there, all right. Also waiting. But for what? His muscles knotted, cramped. *Why didn't they do something?* A quick, stabbing blow would be merciful relief . . . but it did not come.

The Enemy had never been merciful. There was something else they were going to do.

When it came, it was almost overpowering in its intensity. Not hostility, nor anger, nor hatred, as before. Instead, incredibly, a soft gentle mist of supplication, a wave of reproach insinuating itself in his mind. *Why do you hate us when we want only peaceful contact with you? Why do you try to drive us back? We have come from so far, and now you try only to destroy us.*

It caught him off guard. He tried to formulate an answer, but they swept in swiftly, surrounding him with wave after wave of reproach. As always, he could not tell *how* this contact with the Enemy was made. Perhaps they, too, had Analogues. He simply felt them, deep in his mind, and they were closer now, all about him, sucking him deep into their minds. He felt a glowing warmth there now that was utterly different from before. He felt himself drawn, moving slowly, then faster and faster, in tightening spirals toward the vortex as the Enemy's minds drew him in. *We want to stop this fighting, but you prolong it. Why? Why won't you give us a chance?*

For the first time he saw the physical images of the Enemy. They were approaching him on the surface. He couldn't see them clearly . . . only fuzzy outlines . . . but enough to see that they were humanoid, manlike. They moved toward him as he watched. His heart roared with sudden excitement. Could they mean it? Could they really want to reveal themselves, establish contact, put an end to this grueling, brutal Idiot War that had been going on for so long?

Something in his own mind called out a warning, shrieking an alarm. *Don't be a fool! They're treacherous, there's nothing they won't try. Don't let them poison you, fight back!*

He caught at the grips, trying to center his mind on the approaching emissaries, trying to catch the fringes of thought that lay beneath the surface, but the wave of reproachfulness came back at him with increasing intensity.

Why do you hate us so much?

He knew, coldly, what he had to do. It was the only thing to do, even though it seemed so horribly wrong.

He waited until the emissaries were close. Then he struck out at their minds, as viciously as he knew how. He drove the blow home with six long months of bitterness and hatred behind it, striking out wildly, slicing them down like wheat before a scythe. He felt them recoil and crumble, and he pressed his advantage coldly, flailing at the insidious supplicating pattern of thought surrounding him.

The spiral broke, suddenly, releasing him, but this time there was no stark, brutal core of malignancy that he had glimpsed beneath their illusions so many times before. Instead, the vortex receded gently, regretfully . . . injured, bewildered, helpless to understand.

Why? Why will you not even give us a chance? Why do you hate us so much?

It was harder to bear than naked savagery. Frantically Provost rang for Relief. It seemed, suddenly, as if all the wrongs and imagined wrongs he had done in his whole life were welling up to torment him; he knew it was only Enemy illusion, but his mind was screaming, twisting in on itself. A sense of guilt and self-loathing swept through him in waves as he fought to maintain the tiny thread of control. *Butcher!* his own mind was screaming at him. *What kind of monster are you? What if they were sincere? What if you were the one who was wrong?*

The Control board jerked him back before he broke, snapped off his Analogue contact abruptly. He stood up in the darkness of the cubicle and disengaged his cramped hands from the grips. It was over; he was safe. His Rehab conditioning cut in now to take over . . . now there would be Relief from the onslaught, quietness, gentleness, childhood memories, peace. . . .

But the waves of guilt were still washing at his mind. He started walking down the corridor toward the Relief room as his hands began to tremble; then he broke into a run. He knew that only seconds now stood between him and sanity, and sanity lay at the end of the corridor.

The Turner girl was in the room waiting for him. There was soft music, gentle light. She sat across the room, and suddenly he was a five-year-old again, bewildered and overwhelmed by the frightening world around him, desperate for comfort, affection, reassurance. He hurled himself onto the recliner, felt the Turner girl's fingers gently stroking his forehead as he let himself go completely, let great sobs of relief erupt from his throat and shake his shoulders.

She was silent for a long time as his knotted muscles began to relax. Then she leaned forward, bent her lips to his ear.

"Butcher!" she whispered.

Only a whisper, but virulent, malignant. "Toad! You call

yourself human, but you go down there to butcher them! *Monster!"*

Provost screamed. He threw himself back against the wall, arms outstretched, clawing at it and screaming as he stared at her in horror. She faced him, and spit at him, and burst out in mocking laughter as his screams rose from torment to agony.

An alarm bell was clanging now; the girl's lips twisted in revulsion. She threw open the corridor door. *"Butcher!"* she hurled back at him once more, and broke for the door.

Gunfire rattled from both ends of the corridor. The crossfire caught her, lifted her off her feet and dropped her in a crumpled heap on the metal floor plates.

Provost huddled in the corner of the room, babbling.

2   THE ENORMITY of the blow did not register immediately. Like any warfare operation, the Satellite ship was geared to face emergencies; the sheer momentum of its battle station procedure delayed the impact for hours. Then, slowly, the entire operation of the Satellite ship began to freeze in its tracks.

What had happened was no ordinary emergency.

To Dorie Kendall the full, terrifying implication was clear from the start. She had long months of Department of Psychology training behind her at the Hoffman Center, weeks of work with the very men who had developed the neuromolecular Analogues that were Earth's only weapon in this war. Even then, the training had not stopped; on the long passage out from Earth she had continued with days and nights of tape-study and hypno-sleep to prepare her for this crucial assignment. She herself had never been in Analogue contact with the Enemy, but she knew a great deal about the Enemy and what the Enemy might do. The instant Dr. Coindreau, the Satellite surgeon, had called her down to the autopsy, she realized what had happened.

Only now it was dawning on her, in a cold wash of horror, that it was very possibly her own fault that it had happened at all.

"But why don't you *attack* them?" she had asked John Provost a few hours before his shift was to begin. "Why do you always take the defensive?"

Provost had looked at her, patiently, as though she were a child who didn't quite understand the facts of life. "They're perceptive," he said. "They're powerful. Incredibly powerful."

"All the more reason to hit them hard," she had argued. "Hit them with a blow that will drive them back reeling."

Provost smiled. "Is that the new DepPsych theory?"

"All DepPsych knows is that *something* has to be changed. This war has gone on and on."

"Maybe after a while you'll understand why," he had said slowly. "How can we hit them with this powerful blow you talk about when they're busy driving mental javelins into us with all the force they can muster? I can try, but I don't know how to do it."

Well, he had tried, all right, the psychologist reflected, and now bare hours later Provost was strapped down screaming and shattered in one of the isolation cubicles, and the Relief girl. . . .

She watched Dr. Coindreau's lean face and careful fingers as he worked at the autopsy table. Every room in Medical Section, every fixture, had a double use. Sick bay and Rehab quarters. Office and lab. Examining room doubling as surgery. Now it was doubling as morgue. She peered down at the remains of the Turner girl in growing anger and revulsion and wondered, desperately, how the Enemy had managed to do it.

She realized, coldly, that it was up to her to find out how, and fast.

The Enemy had poisoned the Turner girl, somehow. They had reached into the heart of the Satellite ship and struck at the most critical link in the chain—the Relief program that enabled the men to go back into battle.

Without Relief, there could be no men to fight.

But why did we have to murder her? the Kendall girl thought bitterly. *If we could have studied her, we might have learned how the Enemy had done it.*

The blinker over the door flashed, and a big heavy-set man stepped into the room. She recognized Vanaman, commander of the Satellite ship. She had talked to him briefly before. It had been an unpleasant interview; Vanaman had made it quite clear that he could not understand why DepPsych insisted upon sending women out to Saturn Satellite, nor why Earth Control chose *now* of all times to shift gears and saddle him with Dorie Kendall, intent on finding some new approach to the fighting. The big man glared at her, and then stared down at the thing on the table.

"The Turner girl?" he asked the surgeon.

"What's left of her," Dr. Coindreau said. "I'm about finished. It's not going to help us any."

"It's *got* to help us." Vanaman's voice was harsh.

Dorie Kendall looked up at him sharply. "Your trigger happy firing squad didn't leave us much to work with, you know."

Vanaman's fist clenched on the table. Deep-cut lines sliced from his nose down to the corners of his mouth. His face showed the grueling pressure of months of command, and he seemed to control himself only with difficulty. "What did you expect them to do?" he said. "Give her a medal?"

The girl flushed. "They didn't have to kill her."

Vanaman blinked at her. "They didn't, eh? You've been helping the doctor here do the post?"

"Certainly."

"And you've run a standard post-mortem brain wash?" He nodded toward the neuromolecular analyzer clicking in the wall, the great-grandfather of all Analogues.

"Of course."

"And what did you find, Miss Kendall?"

"Nothing intelligible," she said defiantly. "The Enemy had her, that's all."

"Fine," said Vanaman. "And you're standing here suggesting that we should have had *that* running around *alive* on this ship? Even for ten seconds? We know they had her tongue, they must have had her eyes also, her ears, her reason." He shook his head. "Everything we've done against the Enemy has depended on keeping them *away* from us, *off* this ship. That's why we monitor every move of every man and woman here, Miss Kendall, including yourself. That's why we have guns in every corridor and room. That's why we used them on the Turner girl."

There was silence for a moment. Then the doctor pushed back from the table and looked up. "I'm afraid you used them too late on the Turner girl," he said to Vanaman.

"You mean Provost is dead?"

"Oh, no." The doctor jerked off his mask, ran a lean hand through his hair. "He's alive enough. That is to say, his heart is beating. He breathes. Just what is going on above his ears is something else again. I doubt if even Miss Kendall could tell you that. I certainly can't."

"Then he's a total loss." Vanaman's face seemed to sag, and Dorie realized suddenly how heavily the man had been hanging on the thread of hope that Provost might only have suffered minor harm.

"Who can say?" the doctor said. "You take a fine chunk of granite and strike precisely the right blow, precisely hard enough at precisely the right angle, and it will shatter into a dozen pieces. That is what has happened to Provost. Any salvage will be strictly up to DepPsych. It's out of my province." The surgeon's dark eyes met Dorie's for a moment, and shifted away. "Unfortunately, the significance of this attack is greater than the survival or loss of John Provost. We might as well face that right now. The job the Enemy has done on Provost was a precision job. It can mean only one thing: that somehow they have managed to acquire a very complex understanding of human behavior patterns. Am I right, Dorie?"

She nodded. "It isn't *what* they did to Provost that matters so much," she said, "although that's bad enough. It's *how* they did it that matters."

"Then how *did* they do it?" Vanaman asked, turning on her. "That's what you're here for, isn't it? This isn't a war of muscle against muscle or bomb against bomb. This is a war of mind against mind. It's up to the Department of Psychology and the Hoffman Center psych-docs to tell us how to fight this Enemy. Why don't you know?"

"I need time," she said. "I can't give you an answer."

The big man leaned forward, his lips tight across his teeth. "You've *got* to give me an answer," he said. "We can't afford time, can't you see that? This Satellite is the only shield between Earth and the Enemy. If you can't give us the answer, we're through, washed up. We've got to know how they did what they did to Provost."

Through the viewport the pale, yellow globe of Saturn stared up at them, unwinking, like the pale eye of a snake. "I wish I could tell you," Dorie Kendall said. "The Turner girl can't tell us. Neither can Provost. But there may be one way we can learn."

"And that is?"

"Provost's Analogue. It has been the *real* contact with the Enemy. It should know everything Provost knows about them. The Analogue may give us the answer."

3

WITH VANAMAN seated beside her, Dorie fed the tapes from John Provost's Analogue into the playback unit in the tiny projection room in Integration Section. For a few moments, then, she ceased to be Dorie Kendall of DepPsych, trained for duty and stationed on Saturn Satellite, and became John Provost instead.

It was an eerie experience. She realized that every Analogue was different, a faithful impression of the mind of its human prototype; but she had not been prepared for the sudden, abrupt contact with the prototype mind of John Provost.

She felt the sickening thud of his contact with the Analogue just prior to its last descent to the surface. She felt the overwhelming wave of tension and fear that the Analogue had recorded; then the sudden, irrational, almost gleeful sense of elation as John Provost's eyes and ears and mind floated down to the place where the Enemy was. The Analogue tape was accurate to a high degree of fidelity. Dorie Kendall gripped the chair arms until her wrists cramped.

It was like going to the surface herself.

Beside her she was aware of Vanaman's huge body growing tense as he gnawed his knuckles, soaking in the tape record. She felt the growing tension, the snowballing sense of impending disaster reflecting from John Provost's mind.

And then she lost contact with the things around her and

fell completely into Provost's role. The growing supplication of the Enemy surrounded her. She felt the sense of reproach, the helpless appeal of the illusion, and Provost's response, calculated to perfection and deployed like a pawn on a chessboard. *It's a trick, a pitfall, watch out! Don't be fooled, don't fall into their trap. . . .*

She felt the wild fury of Provost's mind as he hurled the illusion aside, struck out at the Enemy as she had told him to do. And then the receding waves of supplication and reproach from the Enemy, and the overwhelming, demoralizing wave of guilt from his own mind—

In that moment she began to understand John Provost, and to realize what the Enemy had done. Her face was pale when the tape stopped. She clenched her fists to keep her hands from trembling.

Vanaman leaned back, defeat heavy on his face. "Nothing," he said. "It's always the same. We have nothing."

"I didn't realize what they could do," Dorie said.

"But that was on the surface. Down there we could fight it, control it. Now they've reached us here, too." The commander stood up and started for the corridor. "For all we know, they've been here all along, just playing with us. We can't really be certain that they haven't. Can you begin to see what we've been fighting, now? We don't know *anything* about them. We can't even be sure we're fighting a war with them."

Dorie Kendall looked up, startled. "Is there any doubt of that?"

"There's plenty of doubt," Vanaman said. "We *seem* to be fighting a war, except that nobody seems to understand just what kind of war we're fighting, or just why we're fighting it." His voice trailed off and he shrugged wearily. "Well, we're backed up to the wall now. Provost was our best Analogue man. He depended utterly on Relief to put him back together again after one of those sessions down there. The Turner girl was the whole key to our fighting technique, and they got to her somehow and poisoned her. If they can do that, we're through."

The girl stared at him. "You mean we should just quit? Withdraw?"

Vanaman's voice was bitter. "What else can we do? Any one of the girls in Relief could be just the same as the Turner girl, right now. They've cracked open our entire strategy in one blow. The Relief program is ruined, and without Relief I can't send another man down there."

"But you've *got* to," Dorie said. "This Satellite is the Earth's only shield. We can't stop now."

"We can't fight them, either. We've been fighting them for months, and we know nothing about them. They come from— somewhere. We don't know where, or when, or how. All we know is what they did to Titan. We're trying to defend ourselves against an imponderable, and our defenses are crumbling." Vanaman closed the tape cans and tossed them into the return file with an air of finality. "Do you know what Provost called this war?"

Dorie Kendall nodded. "He told me. An Idiot War."

"And he was right. *Their* war, not ours. What do they want? We don't know. On *their* choice of battlefield, in *their* kind of warfare, they're whipping us, and we don't even know how. If we had even a glimpse of what they were trying to do, we might be able to fight them. Without that, we're helpless."

She heard what he was saying, and she realized that it was almost true, and yet something stuck in her mind, a flicker of an idea. "I wonder," she said. "Maybe we don't know what the Enemy is trying to do here—but there's one possibility that nobody seems to have considered."

Vanaman looked up slowly. "Possibility?"

"That *they* don't know what they're trying to do, either," Dorie Kendall said.

4 IT WAS A possibility, even Vanaman grudgingly admitted that. But as she went down to Isolation Section to examine John Provost, Dorie Kendall knew that it made no sense, no more nor less than anything else that the Enemy had done since they had come six months before into Earth's solar system.

They had come silent as death, unheralded: four great ships moving as one, slipping in from the depths of space beyond Pluto. How long they had been lurking there, unobserved but observing, no one could say. They moved in slowly, like shadows crossing a valley, with all space to conceal them, intruders in the enormous silence.

An observation post on tiny Miranda of Uranus spotted them first, suddenly and incredibly present where no ships ought to be, in a formation that no Earth ships ever would assume. Instrument readings were confirmed, questioned, reconfirmed. The sighting was relayed to the supply colony on Callisto, and thence to Earth.

Return orders were swift: keep silence, observe, triangulate and track, compute course and speed, make no attempt at contact. But return orders were too late. The observation post on Miranda had ceased, abruptly, to exist.

Alerted patrol ships searched in vain, until the four strange ships revealed themselves in orbit around Saturn. Deliberately? No one knew. Their engines were silent; they drifted like huge encapsulated spores, joining the other silent moons around the sixth planet. They orbited for months. Titan Colony watched them, Ganymede watched them, Callisto watched them.

Nothing happened.

On Earth there were councils, debate, uncertainty; speculation, caution, fear. Wait for them to make contact. Give them time. Wait and see. But the four great ships made no move. They gave no sign of life. Nothing.

Signals were dispatched, with no response. Earth prepared against an attack—a ridiculous move. Who could predict the nature of any attack that might come? Still, Earthmen had always been poor at waiting. Curiosity battled caution and won, hands down. What were these ships? Where did they come from? Hostile or friendly? Why had they come here?

Above all, *what did they want?*

No answers came from the four great ships. Nothing.

Finally an Earth ship went up from Titan Colony, moving out toward the orbit of the intruders. The crew of the contact ship knew their danger. They had a single order: make contact. Use any means, accept any risk, but make contact. Approach with caution, with care, gently, without alarming, but make contact. At any cost.

They approached the intruders, and were torn from space in one instantaneous flash of white light. Simultaneously, Titan Colony flared like an interplanetary beacon and flickered out, a smoking crater three hundred miles wide and seventy miles deep.

Then, incredibly, the four great ships broke from orbit and fled deep beneath the methane and ammonia clouds of Saturn's surface. Earth reeled from the blow, and waited, paralyzed, for the next—and nothing happened. No signal, no sign, nothing.

But now the intruders were the Enemy. The war had begun, if it was a war; but it was not a war that Earthmen knew how to fight. A war of contradiction and wild illogic. A war fought in a ridiculous microcosm where Earthmen could not fight, with weapons that Earthmen did not comprehend.

An Idiot War. . . .

Dorie went to see John Provost just eight hours after the Enemy had struck through the Turner girl. As she followed the tall, narrow-shouldered doctor into the isolation cubicles of Medical Section, he stopped and turned to face her. "I don't think this is wise at all."

"Maybe not," the girl said. "But I have no choice. Provost was closer to the Enemy than anyone else here. There's no other place to start."

"What do you think you're going to learn?" Dr. Coindreau asked.

"I don't know. Only Provost knows exactly what happened in that Relief room."

"We know what happened," the doctor protested. "The Relief room was monitored. Provost had come close to his breakpoint when Control jerked his Analogue back from the surface. The pressure on the men under battle conditions is almost intolerable. They all approach breakpoint, and induced regression in the Relief room is the fastest, safest way to unwind them, as long as we don't let them curl up into a ball."

"You mean it *was* the fastest and safest way," Dorie corrected him.

The doctor shrugged. "They hit Provost at his weakest point. The Turner girl couldn't have done worse with a carving knife. I still don't see what you're going to learn from Provost."

"At least I can see what they've done to him." She looked at the doctor. "I don't see how my seeing him can hurt him."

"Oh, I'm not worried about *him*." The doctor opened the door. At the nursing desk a corpsman was punching chartcards. "How's he doing?" the doctor asked.

"Same as before." Then the corpsman saw the girl. "Doc, you aren't taking *her* in there, are you?"

"That's what she wants."

"You know he's not exactly sold on girls, right now."

"I'll risk it," Dorie said sharply.

Inside the cubicle they found Provost lying on his back on a bunk. The pale blue aura of a tangle-field hovered over him, providing gentle but effective restraint.

Provost was singing.

The words drifted across the room. Dorie suddenly caught them and felt her cheeks turn red.

"Hello, John," the doctor said. "How are you feeling?"

Provost stopped singing. "Fine. Yourself?"

"This is Miss Kendall. She's going to help take care of you."

"Well, now, that's just fine." Provost turned his face toward Dorie. No sign of recognition; his eyes were flat, like a snake's eyes. Impersonal—and deadly. "Why don't you leave us alone to talk, Doc? And turn this tangle-field off. Just for a minute."

She shivered at the tone. Dr. Coindreau said, "John, do you know where you are?"

"In a tangle-field."

"Do you know where?"

Provost ignored the question, stared fixedly at the girl. She had never seen such a malignant stare.

"Do you know what happened to you?" the doctor tried again.

His eyes didn't waver, but he frowned. "Memory's a little sticky. But ten seconds out of this tangle-field would help, I bet." She saw his hand clench on the coverlet until the knuckles whitened.

The doctor sighed. "Listen to me, John. You were on the surface. Something happened down there. What—"

Provost obviously was not listening. "Look, Doc, why don't you cut out of here? My business is with *her,* not you."

"All right, John." Dr. Coindreau turned away. He led the girl back into the corridor. She was no longer blushing. She was dead white and trembling. "You know that he'd kill you before he finished," the doctor said to her gently.

"Yes." She nodded. "I know."

"At least the mechanism is direct enough. Fairly primitive, too. And let's face it, a weaker man would either be dead or catatonic. Provost is a rock of stability in comparison."

She nodded. "But he's turned his hatred on the girl, not on the Enemy."

"It was the girl who hit him, remember?" They stepped into an office, and she took the seat the doctor offered gratefully. "Anyway," he said, "Provost never actually contacted the Enemy. We speak as though he's actually been down on the surface physically, and of course he hasn't. You know how an Analogue works?"

"I ought to—I have one—but I only know the general theory, not the details."

"Nobody knows the details too well, not even your friends at the Hoffman Center. Nobody really could. An Analogue is at least quasi-sentient, and the relationship between an Analogue and its operator is extremely individual and personal. That's precisely why Analogues are the only real weapons we have to use against the Enemy."

"I can't quite see that," Dorie said.

"Look—these creatures, whatever they are—buried themselves on the surface of Saturn and just sat there, right? The blows they struck against Titan Colony and the contact ship showed us the kind of power they *could* bring to bear—but they didn't follow up. They struck and ran. Pretty pointless, wouldn't you say?"

It seemed so, at first glance. Dorie Kendall frowned. "Maybe not so pointless. It made counterattack almost impossible."

Dr. Coindreau nodded grimly. "Exactly the point. We didn't know what—or how—to counterattack. We practically *had* to do *something*, and yet there was nothing we could do."

"Why didn't we land and hunt them out?" the girl asked. "We can get down there, can't we?"

"Well, it's *possible,* but it would have been worse than use-less. It would have taken all our strength and technology just to survive down there, let alone do anything else. So we used Analogues, just the way Grossman and his crew used them to explore the surface of Jupiter. The Analogues were originally developed to treat paranoids. The old lysergic acid poisons had proved that a personality could dissociate voluntarily and reintegrate, so that a psych man could slip right into a para-noid fantasy with his patient and work him on his own ground. Trouble was that unstable personalities didn't reintegrate so well, which was why so many people blew up in all directions on LSD." Dr. Coindreau paused, chewing his lip. "With Ana-logues, the dissociation is only apparent, not real. A carbon copy, with all the sensory, motor, and personality factors out-lined perfectly on protein-molecule templates. The jump from enzyme-antagonists to electronic punched-molecule impres-sions isn't too steep, really, and at least the Analogues are predictable."

"I see," Dorie Kendall said. "So the operatives—like Provost —could send their Analogues down and explore in absentia, so to speak."

"As a probe, in hope of making contact with the Enemy. At least that was the original plan. It turned out differently, though. That was what the Enemy seemed to be waiting for. They drove back the first probers with perfectly staggering brutality. We struck back at them, and they returned with worse. So pretty soon we were dancing this silly gavotte with them down there, except that the operatives didn't find it so silly. Maybe the medieval Earth wars seemed silly, too, with the battleground announced in advance, the forces lined up, the bugles blowing, parry and thrust and everybody quits at sunset. But lots of men got killed that way just the same." He paused for a moment, wrapped in his own thoughts, and then went on with sudden firmness: "There was no sense to this thing, but it was what the Enemy seemed to want. And our best men have thrown everything they could into it, and only their conditioning and the Relief room has kept them going."

"Weren't Psi-Highs used for a while?" Dorie said.

"Yes, but it didn't work. The Enemy is not telepathic, for one thing, or at least not in the sense we think of it; and anyway, the Psi-Highs couldn't keep themselves and their Analogues separated. It was pure slaughter, for them, so they were pulled back to Earth to help build the Analogues for psi-negatives to use." He shot a glance toward the cubicle. "Well, now that's all over. No Relief, no Analogues. The Enemy has simply shifted the battle scene on us, and we're paralyzed."

For a long moment the DepPsych girl sat in silence. Then she said, "I don't think 'paralyzed' is exactly the word you want. You mean 'panicked'."

"Does it make any difference?"

"Maybe a world of difference," the girl said thoughtfully, *"to the aliens."*

5

PARALYSIS OR PANIC, the effect on the Satellite ship was devastating.

Twelve hours after Provost was dragged kicking and screaming out of the Relief room, the ship's crew waited in momentary anticipation, braced against the next blow. They could not guess from where it might come, nor what form it might take. They could only sit in agony and wait.

Twenty-four hours later, they still waited. Thirty-six hours, and they still waited. Activity was suspended, even breathing was painful. In the day room the Analogue operatives gnawed their knuckles, silent and fearful, unwilling to trust even a brief exchange of words. They were Earthmen, the girl realized, and Earthmen were old hands at warfare. They understood too well the horrible power of advantage. Earthly empires had tottered and fallen for the loss of one tiny advantage.

But the Enemy's advantage was not tiny. It was huge, over-powering. The men here could only wait for the blow to fall. It *had* to fall, if there were order and logic in the universe.

It didn't fall. They waited, and far worse than a brutal, concerted attack against them, nothing happened.

The paralysis deepened. The Enemy had reached a girl within the Satellite and turned her into a murderous blade in their midst. Who could say how many others had been reached? No one knew. There was nothing to grasp, nothing to hold on to, *nothing*.

Dorie Kendall did not elaborate on her remark to Dr. Coindreau, but something had slid smoothly into place in her mind as she had talked to him, and she watched the Satellite and its men around her grinding to a halt with a new alertness.

The attack on Provost through the Turner girl was not pointless, she was certain of that. It had purpose. Nor was it an end in itself. It was only the beginning. To understand the purpose it was necessary somehow to begin to understand the Enemy.

And that, of course, was the whole war. That was what the Enemy had so consistently fought to prevent. *They have built up an impenetrable wall, a blinding smokescreen to hide themselves,* she thought, *but there must be some way to see them clearly.*

The only way to see them was through Provost. She was certain of this, though she wasn't sure why. She went to the isolation cubicle to see him again, and then again and again. It was unrelieved torment for her each time; for all her professional training, she had never before encountered such a malig-

nant wall of hatred. Each time his viciousness and abusiveness
seemed worse as he fought against the restraining tangle-field,
watching her with murderous hatred; she left each time almost
physically ill, and whenever she slept she had nightmares. But
again and again she worked to break through his violent obses-
sion, more and more convinced that John Provost was the key.
They were brutal interviews, fruitless—but she watched as
she worked.

Vanaman found her in Medical Section on the third day,
a red-eyed, bitter Vanaman, obviously exhausted, obviously
fighting for the last vestige of control, obviously helpless to
thwart the creeping paralysis in the ship under his command.
"You've got to hit Eberle with something," he said harshly.
"I can't make him budge."

"Who is Eberle?" the girl wanted to know.

"The Analogue dispatcher. He won't send an Analogue
down."

"I thought you weren't going to."

"I've *got* to do *something,* Relief or no Relief, but Eberle
is dragging his feet."

She found John Eberle in the Analogue banks, working by
himself, quietly and efficiently and foolishly, testing wires,
testing transmission, dismantling the delicate electronic units
and reassembling them in an atmosphere of chaos around him.
The operative cubicles were empty, the doors hanging open,
alarm signals winking unheeded.

"What are you doing with them?" Dorie asked, staring down
at the dismantled Analogues.

Eberle grinned foolishly. "Testing them," he said. "Just
testing."

"But Vanaman says we need them down on the surface *now*.
Can't you see that?"

Eberle's smile faded. "I can't send them down there."

"Why not?"

"Who's going to operate them?" the dispatcher asked. "What will the operators do for Relief?" His eyes narrowed. "Would *you* want to take one down?"

"I'm not trained to take one down. But there are operators here who are."

Eberle shrugged his shoulders. "Well, you're DepPsych, maybe you've got some magic formula to make the men go down without any Relief to count on. I can't make them. I've already tried it."

She stared at him, and felt a wave of helplessness sweep over her. It was as though she were standing in an enormous tangle-field, and all her efforts to free herself only settled it more firmly on her shoulders. She knew it wasn't anything as simple as fear or cowardice that was paralyzing the ship.

It was more than that, something far deeper and more basic.

Once again she was forced back to where it had all started, the only possible channel of attack.

John Provost. She headed for the isolation cubicle.

Thirty-six hours, and she had barely slept; when exhaustion demanded rest, her mind would not permit it, and she would toss in darkness, groping for land, for something solid to grasp and cling to.

Provost sucked up most of her time—wasted hours, hours that drained her physically and emotionally. She made no progress, found no chink in the brutal armor. When she was not with him she was in the projection booth, studying the Analogue tapes stored and filed from the beginning, studying the monitor tapes, watching and listening, trying somehow to build a composite picture of this enigmatic Enemy that had appeared from the depths of space, struck, and then drawn back to the inaccessible surface of Saturn. There were too many pictures, that was the trouble. None of them fit. None corresponded to the others. She was trying to make sense from nonsense, and always the task seemed more hopeless than before.

And yet, slowly, a pattern began to emerge.

An alien creature, coming by intent or accident into a star system with intelligent life, advanced technology. The odds were astronomical against its ever happening. Probably not a truly unique occurrence in the universe, but very possibly unique for these alien creatures.

What then?

A pattern that was inevitable. . . .

She answered a violent summons from Vanaman. He demanded progress with John Provost, and she told him there was no progress. He paced the floor, lashing out at her with all the fury that had been building up as the hours had passed. "That's what you're here for," he told her harshly. "That's why we have DepPsych—to deal with emergencies. We've got to have progress with that man."

Dorie Kendall sighed. "I'm doing everything I can. Provost has a good, strong mind. He has it focussed down on one tiny pinpoint of awareness, and he won't budge it from there."

"He won't!" Vanaman roared. "What about *you?* You people are supposed to have techniques. You can break him away from it."

"Do you want him dead?" she asked. "That's what you'll get if I drive him too hard. He's clinging to his life, and I mean that literally. To him, I am the Turner girl, and all that is sustaining him is this vicious drive to destroy me, as quickly as he can, as horribly as he can. You can use your imagination, I think."

Vanaman stared at her. She met his haggard eyes defiantly. Vanaman broke first. It was almost pitiable, the change; he seemed to age before her eyes. The creases in his face seemed to harden and deepen, and his heavy hands—threatening weapons before—fell limp. Like a spirited dog that had been whipped and broken by a brutal master, he crumbled. "All right. I can't fight you." He spread his hands helplessly. "You know that I'm beaten, don't you? I'm cornered, and there's no place to turn. I know why Provost dreaded those long waits between shifts now. That's all I can do—wait for the blow to fall."

"What blow?" said the girl.

"Maybe you can tell me." A strangled sound came from Vanaman's throat. "Everything we've done against them has been useless. Our attempt to contact them, our probing for them and fighting them on the surface—useless. When they got ready to hit us here, they hit us. All our precautions and defenses didn't hinder them." He glared at her. "All right, you tell me. What is it we're waiting for? When is the blow coming? From where?"

"I don't think there's going to be any blow," said Dorie Kendall.

"Then you're either blind or stupid," Vanaman snapped. "They've driven a gaping hole in our defenses. They know that. Do you think they're just going to let the advantage slide?"

"Human beings might not, but they're not human beings. You seem to keep forgetting that."

Words died on Vanaman's lips. He blinked and frowned. "I don't follow you," he said after a moment.

"So far, everything they've done fits a pattern," Dorie said. "They have physical destructive power, but the only times they've used it was to prevent physical contact. So then after they struck, what did they do? Press forward? Humans might, but they didn't. Instead, they moved back to the least accessible geographical region they could find in the solar system, a planetary surface we could not negotiate, and then they waited. When we sent down Analogue probers, they fought us, in a way, but what has made that fight so difficult? Can you tell me?"

"The fact that we didn't know what we were fighting, I suppose," Vanaman said slowly. "The Analogue operatives didn't know what was coming next, never two attacks the same."

"Exactly," said the girl. "They knocked us off balance and kept us there. They didn't use their advantage then. Everything was kept tightly localized until the Analogue operatives began to get their feet on the ground. You saw the same tapes I did. Those men were beginning to know what they were doing down there; they knew they could count on their conditioning and the Relief rooms to keep them from breaking, no matter how powerful the onslaught. So now, *only now,* the Enemy has torn that to ribbons, through the Turner girl." She smiled. "You see what I mean about a pattern?"

"Maybe so," Vanaman conceded, "but I don't see why."

"Look—when you poke a turtle with a stick, what happens? He pulls in his head and sits there. Just that one little aggressive act on your part gives you a world of information about how turtles behave. You could write a book about turtles, right there. But suppose it happened to be a snapping turtle you poked, and he took the end of the stick off. You wouldn't need to poke him a second time to guess what he would do, would you? You already know. Why bother with a second poke?"

"Then you're saying that the Enemy won't strike again because they have what they want," said Vanaman.

"Of course," the girl said bleakly. "They have Provost. Through Provost they have every mind on this Satellite. They don't need to fight on the surface any more, they're right here."

Vanaman's eyes were hard as he rose from his seat. "Well, we can stop that. We can kill Provost."

She caught his arm as he reached for the intercom switch. "Don't be ridiculous," she said tightly. *"What do you think you're going to do when you've killed him?"*

"I don't know," he snarled. "But I'll do something. I've got to get them out into the open somehow, out where I can see them, before we *all* split open at the seams."

"You mean find out whether they have green skins and five legs or not? Who cares?" She twisted his arm with amazing strength, pushing him back into the seat. "Listen to me, you fool. What we have to know is what they want, how they think, how they behave. Physical contact with them is pointless until we know those things. Can't you see that? *They've realized that from the start.*"

He stared at her. "But what do *you* think we should do?"

"First, find out some of the things we have to know," she said. "That means we have to use the one real weapon we've got—John Provost—and I'm going to see that he's kept alive. Show me your arm."

Puzzled, Vanaman held it out to her. The needle bit so quickly he could not pull back. Realization dawned on his face.

"Sorry," she said gently. "There's only one thing we can do, and killing Provost isn't it." She pushed him back in the seat like a sack of flour. "I wish it were," she added softly, but Vanaman wasn't listening any more.

6

As she moved down the corridor the magnitude of what she was doing caught Dorie and shook her violently. Things had crystallized in her mind just before she had gone to talk with Vanaman. A course of action had appeared which she only grasped in outline, and she had moved too fast, too concisely, before thinking it out in full. But now she had tripped the switch. The juggernaut was moving in on her now, ponderously, but gaining momentum.

There would be no stopping it now, she knew, no turning it back. A course of action, once initiated, developed power of its own. She was committed. . . .

Earth was committed. . . .

She shook off that thought, forcefully. She was too terrified to think about that aspect of it. Her mind was filled and frozen by the ordeal she knew was facing her now: John Provost.

Somehow she had to take Provost back from them, wrench him out of their grasp. She remembered the hard, flat look in his eyes when he watched her, and she shuddered.

There was a way to do it.

All around her she could feel the tension of the Satellite ship, waiting helplessly, poised for demolition. She ran down the empty corridors, searched the depths of the ship until she found the place she was seeking. Once inside Atmosphere Control section she leaned against the wall, panting.

Then she slipped the filters into her nostrils, and broke the tiny capsules, feeding them into the ventilation ducts of the ship.

She would take Provost back from the Enemy; then, if she survived—what? There were only hazy outlines in her mind. She knew the limitation of thought that was blocking her. It was the limitation that was utterly unavoidable in thinking of an alien, a creature not of Earth, not human. The limitation was so terribly easy to overlook until the alien was there facing her: the simple fact that she was bound and strapped by a human mind. She could only think human thoughts, in human ways. She could only comprehend the alien insofar as the alien possessed *human* qualities, not an inch further. There was no way she could stretch her mind to cope with alien-ness. But worse—even in trying desperately to comprehend alien-ness, her own human mind inevitably assumed a human mind on the part of the alien.

This the Enemy did not have. What kind of mind the Enemy did have she could not know, but it was not a human mind. Yet that alien mind *had* to be contacted and understood.

It had seemed an insoluble conundrum—until she had realized that the Enemy had faced exactly the same problem, and solved it.

To the Enemy, stumbling upon intelligent life in Earth's solar system, a human mind was as incomprehensible as an alien mind was to a human. *They* had faced the same dilemma, and found a way to cope with it. *But how?* The very pattern of their approach showed how. It was data, and Dorie Kendall had treated it as data, and found the answer.

It revealed them.

They tried so hard to remain obscure while they studied us, she thought as she moved back toward the Analogue Section, *and yet with every move they made they revealed themselves to us further, if we had only had the wit to look. Everything they did was a revelation of themselves. They thought they were peering at us through a one-way portal, seeing us and yet remaining unseen, but in reality the glass was a mirror, reflecting their own natures in every move they made. They discovered our vulnerability, true, but at the same time inadvertently revealed their own.*

The ventilators hummed. She felt the tension in the ship relaxing as the sleep-gas seeped down the corridors. Muscles uncoiled. Fear dissolved from frightened minds. Doors banged open; there was talking, laughter; then lethargy, dullness, glazed eyes, yawns, slack mouths—

Sleep. Like Vanaman, slumped back in his chair, everyone on the Satellite slept. Operatives fell forward on their faces. The girls in the Relief rooms yawned, dozed, snored, slept.

It seemed to Dorie that she could sense Provost's thoughts

twisting out toward her in a tight, malignant channel, driving to destroy her, seeking release from the dreadful hatred the aliens were using to bind him. But then even Provost dozed and slept.

With the filters protecting her, she was alone on the ship, a ghost. In the Analogue bank she activated the circuits she needed, set the dials, rechecked each setting to make certain that she made no error.

She dared not make an error.

Finally, she went to Provost. She dragged his drugged body into the Analogue cubicle and strapped him down. She fit his hands into the grips. Another needle, then, to counteract the sleep-gas, and his eyes blinked open.

He saw her and lunged for her with no warning sound. His arms tore at the restraints, jerking murderously. She jumped back from him a little, forcing out a twisted smile. She reached out mockingly to stroke his forehead, and he tried to bite her hand.

"Butcher!" she whispered. "Monster!"

Pure hate poured from his mouth as she laughed at him. Then she threw the Analogue switch. He jerked back as contact was made, and she moved swiftly to her own Analogue helmet waiting in the adjacent cubicle, threw another switch, felt in her own mind the sickening thud of Analogue contact.

Her Analogue. A therapeutic tool before, now a deadly weapon in frightened, unsteady hands.

She was afraid. It seemed that she was watching images on a hazy screen. She saw Provost there, facing her, hating her, but it was only a mental image. She was sitting alone in darkness and knew that he also was sitting in darkness. Then gradually the darkness seemed to dissolve into unreality; the two Analogue images—hers and Provost's—became sharp and clear.

It was like a dream, a waking nightmare. Provost was moving in on her slowly, his mouth twisting in hatred, great knots of muscle standing out in his arms. He seemed to tower over her for a moment in vicious anticipation. She screamed and broke down the corridor. He was after her like a cat. He leaped, struck her legs, threw her down on the metal floor and fell on her. She saw his arm upraised, felt the fist crash down again and again and again. Broken flesh, broken bones, paste, pulp, again and again. And in the dark Analogue cubicle she seemed to feel every blow.

She closed her eyes, her control reeling. There would be no Relief for her later, she knew that. She fought him, then abandoned fighting and just hung on doggedly, waiting for the end.

Abruptly, he was gone. She had felt his release as his hatred had burned itself out on her. He had stopped, and stood still, suddenly mild, puzzled, tired, wondering as he looked down at the thing on the floor. And then. . . .

She knew he had started for the surface.

7 To Provost it was like awakening from warm and peaceful sleep into terror.

He was horrified and appalled to realize that he had been sleeping. What had happened? Why didn't Control respond? Frantically he seized the hand grips, drove his Analogue down toward the surface. In his mind were fragments of memory. Something hideous had happened, long long ago, something in the Relief room. Afterwards he had been held down in a tangle-field, and time after time the Turner girl had come back to him in the isolation cubicle—or *had* it been the Turner girl?

Then just now he had found her and the tangle-field was gone, and the hideous thing had been repeated.

And the horrible, abrupt awakening to the fact that the Satellite ship was utterly helpless and undefended from the Enemy.

How long had he slept? What had happened? Didn't they realize that every passing second might be precious to the Enemy, fatal to the Satellite?

He felt someone following him, screaming out at him in alarm. Not the Turner girl, as he had thought, but Dorie Kendall, the DepPsych agent, following him down to the surface with her own Analogue.

Provost hesitated, fighting the sense of urgency in his mind. "Don't stop me," he told her. "I've got to get down there. There's no one covering—"

"You can't go down," she cried. "You have no support here. No conditioning, no Relief. We've got to do something very different."

"Different?" He felt her very close to him now and he paused in confusion. What did she know about the Enemy? "What's happening here? The Enemy is down there. *Why have we stopped fighting?*"

She was telling him, frantically, as he groped through his confusion and tried to understand. "They had to know if we had a vulnerability, *any* vulnerability. Something they could use against us to protect themselves if they had to. They knew they could never risk direct contact with us until they knew that we were vulnerable in some way."

Provost shook his head, uncomprehending. "But why not?"

"Try to see *their* view," she said. "Suppose we were hostile, and invulnerable. We might not stop at destroying their ships, we might follow them home and destroy them there. They couldn't know, and they couldn't take a risk like that. They had to find a vulnerability to use as a weapon before any contact was possible. So they drew us out, prodded us, observed us, trying to find out limitations—if we had any. And they discovered our vulnerability—*panic*. A weakness in our natures, the point where intelligence deserts us and renders us irrational, helpless to fight any more. This is what they could use to control us, except that they must have the same vulnerability!"

He hesitated. The driving urge to go on down to the surface was almost overwhelming, to grapple with them and try once again to break through their barrier there. "Why should they have the same weakness we have? They're aliens, not humans."

"Because they have been doing *exactly the same thing that we would have done if we had been in their place*. Think, John! In all the star systems they must have searched, no sign of intelligent life. Then, suddenly, a solar system that is teeming with life. Intelligent? Obviously. Dangerous? How could they know? *We* wouldn't have known, would we? What would *we* have done?"

Provost faltered. "Tried to make contact, I suppose."

"Physical contact? Nonsense. We wouldn't have dared. We couldn't possibly risk contact until we knew how they thought and behaved, until we knew for certain that we could defend ourselves against them if necessary, that they had some kind of vulnerability. Once we knew that, the way would be open for contact. But no matter how eager we were for contact, and no matter how friendly they might appear *we would have had to have the weapon to fight them first*. Or take an insane risk, the risk of total destruction."

He understood her, but it didn't make sense. He thought of Miranda outpost, Titan Colony, and shook his head. "It doesn't add up," he said. "What they did here was incredible."

"Only if you assumed that they were hostile," she said softly.

"What about the contact ship, the colony on Titan? They burned them both, blew them to kingdom come."

"Because they had to. They did what we would have done under the same circumstances. They goaded us. Then they took cover and waited to see what we would do. They made us come after them where we couldn't reach them physically, to see what we could do. They deliberately kept one step ahead, making us reveal ourselves every step of the way, until they found the soft spot they were seeking and threw us into panic. What they failed to realize was that they were inevitably mirroring themselves in everything they did."

Silence then. In the dark cubicle, Provost could see the hazy image of the girl in his mind, pleading with him, trying to make him understand. Gradually it began to make sense. "So they have their weapon," he said slowly, "and still we can't make contact with them because *we* have none against *them*."

"*Had* none," the girl corrected him. "But we have seen them in the mirror. Their thoughts and actions and approach have been humanlike. They recognized our panic for what it was when they saw it. How could they have, unless they themselves knew what panic was—from their own experience?"

"And now?"

"We turn the tables," she said. "If they also have a vulnerability, there will be no more barrier to contact. But we don't dare *assume*, we have to *know*. Every time they have goaded us we have reacted. We've got to stop that now. We've got to withdraw from them completely, leave them with nothing to work with, nothing to grasp."

"But the Satellite—"

"The Satellite is dead for the time being, asleep. There's no one here but us for them to conatct. Now we have to withdraw too. If we do that, can't you see what *they* will have to do?"

Slowly he nodded. He sensed that she hadn't told him all of it, but that, too, was all right. Better that there be *nothing* that the Enemy could draw from his mind. "You tell me what to do, and when," he said.

"Close your mind down, as completely as you can. Barricade it against them, if you can. Keep them out, leave nothing open for them to probe. Cut them off cold. But be ready when I signal you."

He twisted in the cramped seat in the cubicle, clamping down his control as he felt Dorie clamping down hers. It was an exercise in patience and concentration, but slowly he felt his mind clearing. Like a rheostat imperceptibly dimming the lights in a theater, the Satellite went dimmer, dimmer, almost dead. Only a flicker of activity remained, tiny and insignificant.

They waited.

It might have been hours, or even days, before the probing from the Enemy began. Provost felt it first, for he had known it before, tiny exploratory waves from the alien minds, tentative, easy to strike away. He caught himself just in time, allowed himself no response, trying to make his mind a blank grey surface, a sheet of nothing.

More probing then, more urgency. Sensations of surprise, of confusion, of concern. Unanswered questions, fleeting whispers of doubt in the alien minds. Slowly confusion gave way to doubt, then to fear.

This was something the Enemy clearly had not anticipated, this sudden unequivocal collapse. The probing grew more frantic in its intensity. Deepening of doubt, and then, amazingly, regretfulness, self-reproach, uncertainty. *What has happened? Could we have destroyed them? Could we have driven them too far?*

The probing stopped abruptly. Provost felt the DepPsych girl stir; vaguely his eyes registered the darkness of the cubicle around him, the oval viewport in the wall showing the pale yellow globe of Saturn lying below, its rings spreading like a delicate filigree. . . .

Nothing.

In his own mind he felt a stir of panic, and fought it down.

What if the DepPsych girl were wrong? It was only a human mind which had assumed that creatures which behaved alike were alike. In the silence a thousand alternative possibilities flooded his mind. The minutes passed and the panic rose again, stronger. . . .

Then he saw it in the viewport. Up from the methane clouds they came, slowly, four great ships in perfect formation. They rose and stabilized in orbit, moved again, stabilized, moved again.

They were approaching the Satellite.

He felt his fingers clench on the grips as he watched, his mind leaping exultantly. *She had been right. They were forced out.* The offensive had shifted, and now *the Enemy* were forced to move.

Provost saw with perfect clarity the part the DepPsych girl hadn't told him—the thing he and she were going to do.

They waited until the ships were very close. Then:

"Provost! *Now!*"

They struck out together, as a unit, hard. They hit with all the power they could muster, striking the sensitive alien minds without warning. They could feel the sudden crashing impact of their attack. He could never have done it alone; together their power was staggering. The alien minds were open, confused, defensive; they reeled back in pain and fear—

In panic.

Suddenly the four great ships broke apart. They moved out in erratic courses, driving back for the planet's surface. They scuttled like bugs when a rock is overturned, beyond control and frantic. In a matter of minutes they were gone again, and the silence rose like a cloud from the surface.

8

SOMEWHERE IN the Satellite a bell was ringing. John Provost heard it, dreamily, as he rose and stretched his cramped muscles. He met Dorie Kendall in the corridor, and he could tell from the look on her face that she knew it was over, too.

The aliens were vulnerable. They were vulnerable to the same primitive and irrational defense reactions that humans were vulnerable to when faced with a crisis: the suspension of reason and logic that constituted panic. The knowledge was the weapon that Earthmen needed to make contact possible.

Now each side had a weapon. The mirror had reflected the aliens accurately, and the meaning of the reflection was unmistakably clear. There need be no danger in contact now. Now there could be a beginning to understanding.

Without a word John Provost and the girl began to waken the crew of the Satellite.

Epilogue

SOMEWHERE WITHIN the Watcher's ship a gentle alarm began to chime, more of a dreamlike echo than a sound. The Old One stirred, turned again to the space scanner, as his young companion hurried into the cabin.

"Is it Kadar? At last?"

"Look for yourself," the Old One said.

In the blackness of space between Mars and Jupiter something had appeared on the screen, a faint fluorescent glow that shimmered and faded and then returned more strongly. Soon it was nearer, and the tiny scooter ship seemed to materialize before their eyes. Then, in a deft maneuver, the scooter came abreast and was engulfed by the mother ship, and Kadar had returned to them.

At last.

"No problems?" the Old One asked later, after Kadar had refreshed himself. "Nothing new to add? We can really go?"

"Nothing new," said Kadar. "It was a graceful exit, I might say; no fanfare, no suspicions. And we can go—although I'll miss them, I suppose, after spending so long among them."

179

"And your final impression?"

"The same as before, of course, for a favorable decision. I've known that for decades, just as you have. But even so, we have to go. After all, they don't need us any more."

The Young One, listening dubiously, frowned. "Don't need us? I don't understand."

"You reviewed the records again?" the Old One asked.

"Of course—but I thought we were Watchers only. How could they have *needed* us if we were merely watching? And why was Kadar there so long, posing as one of them in their own Hoffman Center? Have we in fact been doing more than watching? The Covenant forbids contact or interference."

The Old One smiled. "Of course. But *guidance* could be something else again. Especially when a people show such frightening promise. These Earthmen could qualify as Watchers, one day! But the smallest choices now could mean so much, the balance between the right move and the wrong so very delicate. Can a gentle nudge at precisely the right point in time be condemned as interference?"

"Maybe not," the Young One said angrily, "but color it as you will, we still have violated the Covenant. We have been more than Watchers here. We have been teachers and guides as well."

"Not quite," the Old One said. "Protectors, if you insist, seeking now and then to shield them from themselves until no shield was needed. What is their quaint term, Kadar? *Guardian angels.* Every child has one, some of them believe, until he learns to find his way."

"And now?" the Young One said.

"We will be back," replied the Old One, turning to the ship's controls with finality, "but not as guardian angels. Merely to watch the child grow strong and healthy. He has already learned to find his way."